Also by H

Nothing Hidden Ever Stays

Daughters of the Sea

The Remembering Tree

Writing as Heidi Renee Mason

To Have and To Hold (The Vows 1)

For Better or For Worse (The Vows 2)

'Til Death Do Us Part (The Vows 3)

Always Hope

Finding the Invisible Woman

Love At First Crepe (Sweet Escape 1)

Just Double the Recipe (Sweet Escape 2)

For information, contact the publisher, Tangled Tree Publishing.

WWW.TANGLEDTREEPUBLISHING.COM

Editing: Hot Tree Editing

Cover Designer: BookSmith Design

Ebook ISBN: 978-1-922679-23-9

Paperback ISBN: 978-1-922679-24-6

Matthew 27:3-5 Then when Judas, his betrayer, saw that Jesus was condemned, he changed his mind and brought back the thirty pieces of silver to the chief priests and the elders, saying, "I have sinned by betraying innocent blood." They said, "What is that to us? See to it yourself." And throwing down the pieces of silver into the temple, he departed, and he went and hanged himself.

"The redbud is often called the Judas tree, for the betrayer of Christ, who is said to have hanged himself from such a tree, after which the white flowers turned red with blood or shame." -Britannica.com

Foreword

Robert Phoenix, Braucher

Writing about a specific folk cultural tradition is no easy thing. Translating that tradition into a fictional environment for a novel is much more difficult. When Heidi approached me about her book, I was excited to see how she would turn a simple faith healing tradition into something that could come alive through the pages of a book and capture the reader's imagination. Pennsylvania German Braucherei is an old and quiet cultural tradition that relies on faith in the Holy Trinity and the power of the Bible to bring healing and other remedies to the community in need. For the past three hundred years, it has scarcely been heard of outside the rolling hills and farmlands of Pennsylvania. In recent years, however, there is a revival, of sorts, in how folks are viewing their spirituality through a lens of ancestral and cultural heritage, and more and more of those folks are finding their way back to the old traditions that are tried and true. I hope you are as excited as I am to read about the Muller-Ackermann family and how they have managed to keep the Braucherei tradition alive after 300 years and over 3000 miles away from its roots in Pennsylvania. Who knows? Maybe some of that magic will leap off the pages and take root within you. As long as there are folks who keep the old magic alive, our folk cultural traditions will never truly fade into history.

Robert Phoenix
Lemoyne, Pennsylvania

For more information about Braucherei, visit my website at www.PAGermanPowwow.com

Note from the Author

Writing *The Remembering Tree* has been quite a journey for me. Out of all the books I've written, this one has taken the longest. I began writing it in February of 2020, right about the time the world turned upside down as a result of the pandemic. The story idea came at me fast and hard, and I believed this book was practically going to write itself. How wrong I was! I quickly came to realize that, although I had a pretty concrete story idea, none of the details were coming to me. The characters refused to flesh themselves out. I would sit down to write, and the words wouldn't come. The idea was there, and it was good, but it needed time to percolate.

Rather than fight it, I set the manuscript aside—something I never do. I let *The Remembering Tree* rest on the back burner for most of the rest of the year. I came back to it from time to time, hoping to get inspired, but it just wasn't speaking to me. I knew whatever piece was missing would eventually show itself, so I waited.

A few months later, I was scrolling through the internet and came across a story that caught my attention. It was about the 1929 York Hex Murder Trial—a story of one folk healer who killed another when he believed he had been hexed. That was the first time I was introduced to the word Braucherei, and I was intrigued enough to dive down the rabbit hole.

Braucherei is a Pennsylvania Dutch folk healing practice that draws upon the power of God to heal both physical and spiritual illnesses. It is a tradition that has been around for hundreds of years, but it is such an obscure practice that few know of its existence. Having grown up in Ohio, next door to the Pennsylvania Dutch, smack-dab in the middle of Amish and Mennonite communities, I was fully intrigued. I began to search for any and all information I could find on the practice, which led me to Robert Phoenix, a modern-day practitioner of Braucherei.

Something about the practice spoke to me. The traditions and culture weaved their way into my brain and wouldn't let up. I immediately knew the

Braucherei history was the missing piece to the story of *The Remembering Tree*. With this new idea in mind, the novel began to come alive. Following the trail and weaving this lovely, obscure practice into my story was the missing piece I had been waiting for.

I hope you enjoy *The Remembering Tree*. This has been a labor of love for me, and I can't wait to share it with you all.

H.R. Mason

Prologue

Beacon Shores, Washington

"What's that, Mama?"

The little girl scrunched up her forehead and shielded her eyes with her hand, blocking the sunlight.

"It's nothing for you to worry about, child. Go now, run to the shed and bring me the shovel," her mother commanded.

"But, Mama—" the child argued.

"Don't argue with Mama. Go get the shovel," the older sister demanded, sensing their mother wasn't in any mood for her sister's antics.

Stomping her foot angrily, the younger girl opened her mouth to speak but apparently thought better of it. Shaking her head in frustration, she ran behind the house toward the shed.

"This box holds our future. We must bury it immediately," the mother informed her oldest daughter, her voice shaking as she leaned over and placed her empty palms on top of the large trunk sitting at her feet.

"I don't understand, Mama. If that box is our future, why are we burying it?" the daughter questioned.

"Because we must. We don't need it right now, but the time may come when we do. And if anyone finds it, or even knows about it, that will be the end of us."

The mother's green eyes flashed with fear and anger. The daughter's blood ran cold, aware that her all-seeing mother knew far more than she was sharing. Her mama always knew what was coming, and the look in her eyes said it wasn't good.

"I got the shovel, Mama," the younger girl yelled as she rounded the corner of the house carrying the old tool.

"Thank you, my girl," the mother replied with a tight smile as she grabbed the implement from her daughter's hands.

The three took turns digging, upending mounds of dirt as they toiled. When the mother deemed the hole large enough, she and the oldest daughter hefted the unwieldy trunk into the ground. The youngest girl began to toss piles of earth on top, rocks and dirt clattering upon the lid of the strange box.

When the hole was filled, the mother reached inside the pocket of her apron and pulled out three small seeds. She dropped to her knees, placed the seeds deep inside the dirt, buried them, then leaned down and kissed the spot where they lay.

"*Herr Jesu dir leb ich, Herr Jesu dir sterb ich, Herr Jesu dein bin ich todt un lebendig... Lord Jesus, I live to thee, Lord Jesus, I die to thee, Lord Jesus, I am thine, in death and in life...,*" she murmured quietly.

Standing to her feet, the mother held her hands above the spot where she had buried both the box and the seeds. She began to sing.

The little girl had heard her mother's strange songs many times, and she knew most of them by heart. This one, however, was new. She listened closely as the unfamiliar words fell from her mother's lips.

All at once, the mother focused her gaze on the burial spot. Both of her daughters did the same. The younger one caught her breath as a small green sprout began to emerge from the dirt. The sprout continued to grow, and within seconds, the trunk of a tree began to form.

"Mama?" the child questioned.

"Just watch, my girl. Watch and listen," the mother commanded, clutching her worn Bible to her chest.

"I'm watching, Mama. But what am I listening to?" the little girl asked.

"Listen to the voice inside your heart. You'll know what to do."

It wasn't the first time the little girl's mama had told her to listen to that voice. Closing her eyes, the child quieted all the thoughts swirling through her brain. When everything was silent, she opened her heart and began to listen.

The words came slowly, but as they did, she began to sing.

"Listen close and you'll find me,
Buried 'neath the Remembering Tree.
Tucked inside and nestled deep,
Buried 'neath the Remembering Tree.
Hearts of hatred, hearts of greed
Seek the treasure buried deep.
Only she who holds the key
Will unearth the secrets of the Remembering Tree."

The words stopped coming, and the child opened her eyes slowly, gasping when she saw what the words had produced. What was nothing more than three seeds and a pile of dirt moments before had become a fully grown redbud tree, resplendent with lush red blossoms.

The mother's green eyes glistened with tears as a single drop rolled down her cheek.

"May God have mercy on us all," she whispered.

One

Beacon Shores, Washington

Present Day

Gemma Clayborn tried to ignore the hostility floating through the air as she glanced at her fifteen-year-old daughter, Opal. The girl's anger was palpable, occupying the space between them like a living, breathing thing. It swirled there, thickening like a fog as they drove south.

The Clayborns had left their home in Seattle, where Opal had lived all her life, and were nearing Beacon Shores, the small coastal town where they would try to make a new start.

Gemma blinked away tears as she navigated the car along the winding roads leading them closer to their destination. She missed her husband with a force so strong it nearly took her breath away. He'd been gone for a year, and while everyone told her it would get easier, Gemma didn't believe it. The pain was just as sharp as it had been the day he'd suddenly and unexpectedly left her. Gemma hadn't believed it was possible for a healthy man of only thirty-nine years old to die of a massive heart attack, but apparently it was.

Clayton had been with her one minute, and he was gone the next. She hadn't even had the chance to say the things she wanted to say. Of course, she had no idea what she could have said in that split second that would have had any sort of meaning. All she could do was scream.

How could she possibly convey to him how much she loved him? How he had saved her life? How she'd been floundering every second without him? How she didn't even want to go on? No, that wasn't something she could have put into words, even if she'd had the chance.

"Are you hungry, Opal?" Gemma inquired, hoping to break the uncomfortable silence between them.

"No." Opal sneered.

"Okay." Gemma took a deep breath and tried again. "Maybe we can stop once we get into town and grab something for dinner. Your pick."

"I don't want anything," she answered tersely.

"Opal, you're going to have to eat. And there won't be any food at the house," Gemma explained gently.

"Of course there won't be. There isn't anything at that stupid house. Or in that stupid town," Opal spewed.

Gemma took a ragged breath, reminding herself that her daughter was in pain.

"Sweetheart, I hope you'll at least give it a chance. Beacon Shores might surprise you."

"Whatever. It's not like I have any say in any of this anyway. My opinion means nothing."

Opal crossed her arms over her chest, effectively shutting herself off from the world, or at the very least from her mother.

"I know you're angry with me. I know the last year has been the hardest one of your life. I wish I knew another way around this, but I don't," Gemma explained.

"I don't know why we couldn't stay in our own house. You've ripped me away from my school, my friends, everything I love. And you expect me to just be happy about that?" Opal lashed out.

"I don't expect you to be anything, honey."

"Yes you do."

"Opal, we've talked about this. You know we

couldn't stay in our house. I couldn't afford it alone," Gemma clarified, her lip quivering. She blinked fast to keep the tears at bay.

"But why couldn't we have at least stayed in Seattle? Why do we have to go to some stupid town where they probably don't even have Wi-Fi?"

"Beacon Shores is beautiful. And they do have Wi-Fi. As a matter of fact, they're coming next week to install it at the house."

"I hate that stupid house and I haven't even seen it yet," Opal muttered.

"Look, you know the reason we're going there. My grandmother left me the house. It's free. There's also a fund set aside to help me restore it. It's a place we can live that I can afford."

"Whatever."

"All I'm asking is that you give it a chance," Gemma repeated.

"Do I have any choice?" Opal turned her small body away from Gemma, focusing her angry gaze out the passenger side window.

Gemma took a few deep breaths, trying to slow her racing heart. The tension that had taken up residence in the pit of her stomach simmered, gnawing at her like a dog chewing a bone.

The truth was Gemma felt more like Opal than she

would ever admit. She hadn't wanted to sell their home, the place where she and Clayton had raised Opal. She hadn't wanted to leave the comfort of her safe haven, the house where she could feel Clayton's presence in every nook and cranny. She hadn't wanted to quit her job at the newspaper, where she'd worked for seventeen years. She hadn't wanted to say goodbye to her friends and everything familiar.

But she'd had little choice in the matter. None of this was part of the plan.

Gemma couldn't swing the mortgage alone, and the cost of living in Seattle seemed to increase by the day. The fact that her grandmother bequeathed her a house a mere ten days after the unexpected death of her husband felt like a sign, especially considering that she barely knew the woman. Leaving Seattle felt like the right thing to do. She hoped she wasn't wrong. She couldn't afford to make a mistake, not after everything they'd been through.

Gemma had seen recent photos of Moonstone House, and she had visited there as a child, but she was taking a leap of faith in moving. She had tried to stay in contact with her grandmother, Emerald, over the years, but she probably could have done better. Gemma felt guilty that the woman had left her everything when she'd given so little in return.

Of course, it wasn't really Gemma's fault that she barely knew her grandmother. Her own mother, Topaz, had a falling-out with Emerald. Gemma never knew the exact details of what transpired, but Topaz cut all ties with Emerald after that summer. Gemma had penned letters to her grandmother, and Emerald had even written back a few times, but that was the extent of their relationship. She did have memories of Emerald from the summers she stayed with her, up until she was eight. That was the summer that everything changed between her mother and her grandmother.

Gemma had always understood that the problems between the women were her mother's fault. Topaz had a wild streak and a rebel soul, a combination that made her an unreliable and undependable woman. While Topaz had never been cruel, she was mostly oblivious to her daughter's needs, causing Gemma to become the adult in their relationship at a very young age. Gemma knew Emerald didn't approve of the life choices Topaz made, thus the rift between the women.

Topaz was a bit of a nomad, moving around on a whim. Gemma had lived all over the place growing up, and all she'd ever really wanted was roots, a place to call home. Clayton had given her the stability her soul craved. And it had been snatched away from her in an instant.

Even with all of Topaz's eccentricities, Gemma loved her mother fiercely. She'd been heartbroken when Topaz passed away five years earlier from cancer. That left Gemma the next in line to inherit Moonstone House, the home inhabited by the women in her family for over one hundred years.

Gemma was worried about the move but was also excited to see Moonstone House once again. Starting over was something she had never intended to do, but those were the cards she'd been dealt. If she and Opal had any chance to heal their fractured little family, a fresh start was necessary.

Two

Gemma slowed the car to nearly a crawl as the speed limit dropped to twenty-five miles per hour. Her stomach fluttered strangely as she read the sign welcoming them to Beacon Shores. Although she was overwhelmed with sadness and uncertainty, there was also a small flicker of an emotion that, strangely enough, felt like excitement.

"We're here, honey," Gemma said as she gently placed her hand on Opal's arm, shaking her lightly to wake her.

Opal's bright green eyes fluttered open, and for a moment, Gemma caught a glimpse of the sweet little girl who still lived inside the surly teenager her daughter had become. Gemma knew that girl was still there, although buried quite deeply after all that had happened. She hoped the change of scenery and fresh start would draw her to the surface once again.

Opal didn't reply, but Gemma noticed that she sat up in her seat and studied the little town curiously. They passed a grocery store, a small general store, a bakery, an antique store, and a bookstore/coffee shop. There was a diner and pharmacy as well.

Gemma was pleased to spot a hint of a grin on Opal's face as they drove past a little girl and her dog walking down the sidewalk. The child waved to them excitedly, and Opal half-heartedly raised her hand to return the gesture.

"That little one is certainly excited to see us. Maybe she's the town welcoming committee," Gemma offered.

The smile on Opal's face left as quickly as it had come. She crossed her arms over her chest and pulled the hood of her sweatshirt over her long dark curls. Gemma sighed, feeling Opal's wall go up once again.

"I guess that's pretty much the town," Gemma said as they reached the end of Main Street.

"It's so lame. I can't believe we're going to live here," Opal complained.

Choosing to ignore the remark, Gemma continued, "I'm going to go back to the grocery store and grab a few things to get us through the next couple days."

Gemma pulled into an empty parking lot and turned the car around. She headed back the other direction, maneuvered the car into a spot, and turned off the ignition.

"Do you want to come inside with me or wait here?" Gemma asked.

"I'll wait," Opal mumbled.

"If that's what you want. Is there anything specific you want me to get? Speak now or forever hold your peace," Gemma offered.

"Bagels. The cheesy kind if they have them. Orange juice. Oh, and ice cream," Opal listed.

"Mudslide?" Gemma asked with a grin.

"Is there any other kind?" One corner of Opal's mouth turned up ever-so-slightly.

"Nope. I'll be back soon."

Gemma closed the car door, locked it up tightly, and went inside Sunshine Grocers. Looking around, she scanned the store, trying to decipher the layout and get her bearings. Grabbing a cart, she walked quickly through the aisles, grabbing necessities and staples they might need over the next few days. She would make a list and do a more thorough shopping trip once they were settled.

When Gemma had selected the necessary items, she headed to the checkout, shaking her head in disbelief when she discovered there was no one in line—not a single other person.

"We are definitely not in Seattle anymore." She laughed to herself as she placed her items on the belt.

"How is your day going?" the cashier asked politely.

"It's going well. Thank you for asking, Tabitha," Gemma said, glancing at the girl's name tag.

"I haven't seen you in here before. Are you new?" The girl grinned. "I know everyone."

"I just moved here from Seattle."

"Seattle? Wow. Beacon Shores is going to be a big adjustment for you." Tabitha chuckled.

"I'm sure it will be. But I needed a change of scenery, so I'm hoping this will be just the place."

"Which part of town are you going to be living in?" Tabitha asked as she bagged the items.

"Moonstone House. Have you heard of it?"

"Oh. Well, yes, I think most people around here have heard of it."

Tabitha flicked her gaze away quickly. If Gemma didn't know better, she'd say the girl was afraid.

"Is there something wrong with the place?"

"Uh... no... um, it's just that... well, no one has lived there in a really long time."

"I'll be fixing it up. It's belonged to my family for over a hundred years," Gemma explained.

"That's great. Well, anyway, I've lived here my whole life. If you need anything, just ask. Everyone is really helpful, at least for the most part," Tabitha offered.

"Thank you. I appreciate that," Gemma said as she paid for her purchases.

"I'll see you around, I'm sure. This is the only place in town to get groceries," Tabitha told her.

"It was nice meeting you." Gemma waved as she pushed the cart toward her car.

She popped the trunk and loaded the bags into it. Slamming it shut, she pushed her cart to the corral, then returned to the car, opened the driver side door, and started the engine.

"That was fast," Opal said.

"So fast, right? There was no line. I was literally the only customer in the store." Gemma laughed.

"I can't even imagine." Opal shook her head.

"I might not hate grocery shopping so much without the crowds and lines. Maybe this place won't be so bad after all."

"I seriously doubt that," Opal muttered.

Choosing to ignore the remark, Gemma backed out of the space and turned onto Main Street, passing all the same buildings they had already seen as they headed west. She took a left onto Aster Lane, the road that, according to her directions, would lead them to their destination.

Gemma slowed down as the paved road turned into gravel. They saw nothing but fields and forests for about a mile, and just when she thought they must have taken a wrong turn, the gravel ended and a dirt driveway emerged.

"Is this it?" Opal asked, sitting up a little straighter in her seat.

"I think so," Gemma replied uncertainly.

She slowed the car to almost a crawl as they bounced down the rutted dirt driveway. Both sides of the lane were lined with beautiful Sitka spruce dripping with hanging moss and lichen. The forest beyond the driveway was thick and dense, so much so that a person could easily get lost if they wandered in too far.

"What's that sound?" Opal asked, rolling down her window.

"It's the ocean."

Gemma smiled, remembering how she had loved listening to the roar of the waves when she'd stayed at Moonstone House.

"It must be close by, right?" Opal seemed interested for the very first time.

"You could say that. The backyard is basically the ocean." Gemma laughed.

"The beach is right behind the house? You never said that." Opal grinned widely, showing her perfectly straight teeth.

"Didn't I? It must have slipped my mind."

Gemma chuckled mischievously, knowing she had kept that tidbit of information in her back pocket as a surprise for Opal. Her daughter adored the ocean, and she had known how excited Opal would be to discover it was right outside their back door.

"At least there's that. Living beside the water will be cool."

Opal shrugged, trying to appear nonchalant, but Gemma knew her daughter's opinion of the place had just grown by leaps and bounds.

As they rounded the bend, the house came into view, and a huge smile covered Gemma's face as a series of memories surfaced. She remembered sitting with Emerald on the lower porch, her grandmother rocking in the same chair that still remained, while Emerald taught her about flowers and herbs. She also remembered running through the front yard chasing the butterflies that always seemed to be there in abundance.

A warm, soft energy enveloped her, and she felt at peace for the first time since she had said goodbye to Clayton. She had an immediate feeling of coming home.

"The house is actually really cool. It's old and looks like it needs work, but it's pretty," Opal admitted, taking it all in.

Moonstone House was old indeed. Built in 1890, it was a huge two-story farmhouse with wraparound porches on both levels. There were windows on nearly every surface, allowing the sunlight to stream inside. The eaves had decorative carvings of flowers and vines, and although the white paint was peeling off the siding, the house itself was strong and sturdy. No one had lived there for years, so it needed to be entirely renovated. The plumbing and electricity would have to be updated, but it was certainly livable while the work was being done.

"It needs a lot of TLC. The contractor has already been here for a month getting it as ready for us as he could in that amount of time," Gemma replied.

"Is that him?" Opal pointed toward a tall man carrying a ladder around the front of the house.

"I guess so. I've never met him. I've only talked to

him on the phone. I told him we were coming today, although we're arriving much later than I thought. He probably thinks we got lost." Gemma shrugged.

She brought the car to a stop and studied the man in front of her house. He had shaggy white-blond hair and the body of a man who had spent his entire life doing manual labor. He was well-built and muscular, his skin bronzed from working outdoors. He looked inherently capable of fixing any broken thing.

Sliding from the driver seat, Gemma closed the door behind her. Opal followed.

"You must be Gemma," the man said, tossing his hammer on the ground and walking toward them.

"Guilty as charged," Gemma said as a butterfly landed on her shoulder, catching her completely off guard.

"I'm Eric Johnson." He extended his large, calloused, work-worn hand. "I've been waiting for you."

Gemma placed her hand inside his, and a shock of electricity buzzed between them. She had the strangest sense of déjà vu, as if she'd met the man before. He felt far too familiar to be a stranger. If she were a believer in past lives, she would have sworn the two of them had spent a lot of time together in one of them.

Where have I seen this man before? I feel like I know him so well. I feel so connected to him.

Eric's large hand swallowed her small one, and their palms were stuck together by some strange magnetic force. Gemma looked into his eyes, the exact color of the ocean, and she felt like she was drowning. She gasped for air, as though all the oxygen in her lungs had been sucked out.

Beads of perspiration gathered on her upper lip, and her body broke out in a cold sweat. Her ears began to ring as the sound of the waves grew intolerably loud.

Suddenly, it felt like the very swell of the sea was inside her head. Her vision began to blur, and it seemed that someone had jabbed an enormous knife into her forehead, the pain was so intense. Her heart raced, her breath coming much more quickly than it should have been. She tried to speak, but nothing happened. Her head spun, and the ground was far too close. Her vision went black, and her body melted like an ice cube in the sun, puddling onto the grass below.

Three

"Mom, Mom, wake up. Please." Opal's voice echoed somewhere in the distance.

"Gemma," came another voice, a man's. "Gemma, open your eyes. You're all right."

Gemma blinked a few times, glancing around as her daughter's face swam into her line of vision. She moved her hands, feeling prickling blades of grass beneath her palms.

"Wh-what happened? Why am I on the ground?" she stammered, sitting up slowly.

"You passed out," the man said, reaching out to pull her to her feet. "How are you feeling?"

"I'm okay. Did I really pass out?" She shook her head, trying to remember what had happened.

"You did, Mom," Opal answered, worry echoing in her voice.

"I don't remember anything at all. I shook your hand, and then everything just got all fuzzy," she replied, confused.

"You probably need to eat something. Your blood sugar might be low," Opal offered, sounding much wiser than her years. "Plus we've been driving all day."

"Are you sure you're okay?" the man inquired, compassion and worry washing over his handsome face.

"Yeah, I think I am. I feel just fine now."

"You were out for a couple minutes. I was starting to worry that I might need to call someone," he said.

"I know you, don't I? At least I think I do. You're the contractor, right?" Gemma looked at the kind man closely, trying to remember what he'd said his name was.

"I am." He smiled.

"Eric Johnson," she stated as the memory resurfaced. "That's what you told me your name was right before I passed out."

"Guilty as charged." He chuckled.

"Well, Eric Johnson, that was quite an introduction. I mean, do women always fall at your feet?"

Gemma smiled, trying for a joke in order to lighten the moment.

"Not quite like that," he answered with a hearty laugh.

She cleared her throat. "Well, like I started to say, I'm Gemma." She nodded toward her daughter. "And this is Opal, my daughter."

"Nice to meet you both." Eric grinned. "Opal, I'm sure you hear this all the time, but you look like a miniature version of your mother."

"Yeah, I know." Opal rolled her eyes.

"And now you hate me." He laughed.

"I don't know you well enough to hate you," Opal quipped. "Yet."

"This one has spirit. I like that," Eric said to Gemma.

"You have no idea." Gemma laughed.

Opal hated being told that she looked like her mother, but the fact of the matter was that she did. There was no denying it. The two were nearly mirror images of each other, with their shocking green eyes and wild, curly brown hair. Their porcelain skin was nearly translucent, and they both had what could only be described as an "otherworldly" quality about them.

Their slight statures brought to mind the image of a faerie or woodland sprite. People often did a double take when they walked into a room. Gemma had grown used to it over the years, the way people stared at her, but Opal hadn't yet lived long enough to let it roll off her back.

"Do you fix up a lot of old houses like this?" Opal asked Eric, gesturing toward Moonstone House.

"I do. Old houses are kind of my thing. This one has always been a favorite of mine, so I was very happy to get the chance to spruce up the old girl."

"It's so strange. I didn't think I remembered much about this house, but now that I'm here, it feels like only yesterday that I was sitting on that porch with my grandmother," Gemma said.

"When was the last time you visited?" Eric asked.

"I was eight." Gemma chuckled. "So it was definitely not yesterday."

"Some places get under your skin. This is one of them," Eric offered.

"I think you're right," Gemma agreed. "What do you say we take a look around inside, Opal?"

"Whatever. Then I want to check out the ocean."

The two headed to the car to grab their bags, but Eric beat them to it. He insisted on carrying them.

"Is this all you brought? Two bags?" He lifted an eyebrow in question.

"For now. Our moving truck will be here next

week," Gemma answered.

They followed Eric into the house.

"Where would you like these?" he asked.

"You can just drop them in the mudroom for now. We'll have to take a look around and decide which rooms we want," Gemma replied.

"I'll leave you ladies to the tour. I'm going to get back to work," Eric said.

"Thank you."

"I know your things haven't arrived, but all the appliances work, and there's a coffeepot and toaster in the kitchen. I wanted to be sure you had the basics, so I grabbed them when I was in town last week. I know I can't survive without coffee and toast, so I just assume everyone is that way."

"That was so thoughtful of you, Eric. Please, just add it all to the bill."

"No need. Consider them housewarming gifts." He grinned.

Gemma raised an eyebrow. "That is certainly going above and beyond."

He waved her off. "Now, I'm not sure how much you know about fireplaces, so I'm happy to give you a crash course tomorrow if you'd like. There are wall heaters in every room, so you should stay warm if you don't want to make a fire," Eric explained.

“I would love to make a fire, but I know next to nothing about fireplaces, so I’ll probably take you up on the lesson.” Gemma laughed.

“Just let me know when.”

“Thank you so much for everything you’ve done so far. I know it’s a lot,” Gemma admitted.

“The place needs work, but nothing makes me happier than this sort of thing. I’ll be around most every day, so you’ll get tired of seeing me real soon.” Eric laughed as he headed back outside.

“I doubt that,” Opal said with a smirk as soon as he was gone.

“Doubt what?” Gemma questioned.

“I doubt you’ll get tired of seeing Eric anytime soon. He’s really cute—for an old dude.” Opal chuckled.

Gemma shook her head in disbelief, following her daughter into the kitchen. The change that had come over Opal since they’d arrived felt nothing short of miraculous. Her daughter was laughing and making jokes. She actually seemed to like the house, and she was excited to explore the ocean.

Gemma wasn’t going to hold her breath that Opal’s good mood would last, but she intended to enjoy it while it did.

Four

"Mom, this place is way cooler than I thought it would be," Opal said with fascination as they walked into the kitchen."

"It really is. I remember everything about this room so vividly," Gemma gushed.

The large country kitchen had an oversized cooking range, a center island, a quaint little breakfast nook with a fireplace and built-in table, as well as an adjoining den. The floors were made of brick, which was something Gemma had never seen outside of Moonstone House. She took off her shoes and swept one foot over the surface that had been buffed smooth from years of wear. The room was cozy, light, and airy, and Gemma could clearly picture Emerald peeling potatoes at the counter. She blinked twice, feeling as if her eyes were playing tricks on her because the image was so real.

Opal wandered through the kitchen, touching the white walls almost reverently. "The house is so old. It's like you can feel all the people who lived here before. Is that weird?" she asked.

"Not at all. Emerald believed in things like that," Gemma replied.

Opal continued perusing the kitchen, opening cupboard doors and nosing through the pantry before finally making her way to a small door at the bottom of the staircase.

"What's this?" she asked, peering inside.

"It's a jelly closet," Gemma explained. "At least that's what my grandmother called it."

"What's it for?"

"Well, she preserved a lot of fruit. She also used it to store her tinctures and potions," Gemma said.

"Potions? Was she a witch or something?" Opal laughed.

"I don't know what she was, to be honest."

"What do you mean?"

"Well, Emerald was kind of magical," Gemma began. "She was also bilingual, I think. I remember her speaking another language when I was a kid, but I have no clue what it was. She was unique."

"So was Grandma Topaz." Opal laughed. "She claimed to be psychic. I think she was just a weird hippie."

"My mother was definitely something. But Emerald was different. I've never really met anyone like her. She had a sort of 'knowing' about her. Like, she just understood people. She knew what everyone needed. She was really smart about herbs and plants, and she could make home remedies to cure almost anything. She was very wise."

"I didn't think you knew her that well," Opal countered.

"I'd forgotten," Gemma said quietly as she peered into Emerald's empty jelly closet. "But all these memories keep rushing back to me now that I'm here."

"I guess I never really thought about it before, but all the women in our family are named after jewels. Why is that?" Opal asked. "It's kind of weird."

"I honestly don't know why. My mother told me it was a family tradition to name the girls after gems. Just one of those things, I guess."

Opal started to close the door to the jelly closet but then pointed to a very old broom hanging above the inside doorframe of the small alcove. "What's this?"

"Well... it looks like a broom," Gemma answered, wrinkling her forehead in confusion.

"I know that. I mean, why is it hanging on the wall like that?"

Gemma stood on her tiptoes and looked closer. "I have absolutely no idea. But we're going to leave it alone."

They closed the door to the jelly closet and continued the tour of the downstairs, surveying the living and dining rooms, both of which were huge and boasted large fireplaces. The house was sparsely furnished, which was fine considering Gemma's furniture would arrive soon. It would be nice to see her own things in the old space.

Gemma followed Opal up the staircase, the boards creaking a bit beneath their feet. There were four bedrooms upstairs, all extremely spacious. Three were regular bedrooms, and the fourth was a master suite with a fireplace and bathroom.

"I'm guessing the master bedroom is going to be yours, so I'm going to take the first one at the top of the stairs. I really like that old wardrobe in there," Opal decided. "I also love the canopy bed."

"Perfect. I think I'm going to use one of the other bedrooms for my office, and then we'll have one guest room," Gemma agreed.

"The house is huge. And really beautiful. I guess I thought it was going to be some run-down shack," Opal admitted.

"It's a lovely house. I think it will be a good place for us to start over," Gemma added.

Something flickered across Opal's face, an emotion Gemma couldn't quite put her finger on. Whatever it was caused an immediate change in her daughter's temperament. Opal pulled her hood onto her head and crossed her arms over her chest.

"I'm going to check out the ocean. I'll be back later."

Without another word, Opal sprinted down the stairs and out the back door.

Gemma sighed deeply, trying to figure out what had caused the switch to flip so suddenly. Her daughter was in pain, that much was clear. Gemma had to be gentle with her. As much as she wanted to crack Opal open and make her talk, she couldn't push. If she did, she might push her away completely.

Going downstairs, Gemma went to the mudroom to grab their bags. Hanging on the wall above the front door was another ancient-looking broom. She hadn't noticed it earlier, but now that she'd seen two old brooms hanging in two different places, her curiosity was piqued. They had clearly been there for a very long time, and she wondered about their significance.

Shrugging, Gemma grabbed the bags and carried them back upstairs. She tossed Opal's bag on the canopy bed in her room, then carried her own to the master suite. She noticed that all the beds had been recently made up with what appeared to be fresh linens and wondered if that was Eric's doing as well. She had the feeling he was the sort of man who would think to do something like that.

Flopping down onto the large bed, Gemma allowed herself a moment to wallow. Tears coursed down her cheeks, and she gave in to the sobs that she'd been holding back all day. As much as she loved Moonstone House, the fact of the matter was their lives had been turned upside down. She knew they would find their way eventually, but at that very moment, she didn't want to pretend to be strong.

Wiping her face with her palms, Gemma walked across the room to the large bay window. She had an exquisite view of the ocean, so she curled up on the window seat and watched the waves. She saw Opal sitting cross-legged on the sand, doing the same thing.

"I hope your home and your memory will help us heal, Grandma Emerald," Gemma whispered into the quiet of the room.

"This place is in your blood, child. Everything you need is here."

Her grandmother's voice, as clear as the sound of the waves, echoed in the room. Startled, Gemma jumped from the window seat and turned around in a circle. She was certain that her grandmother was in the room. The voice had been too real for her not to be.

Gemma opened the closet doors, looked inside the bathroom, and, even though she felt foolish doing so, checked under the bed. There was no one in the room besides her.

"Grandma, is that you?" she asked quietly.

"Everything you need is here, child," the voice said again.

FIVE

The next morning, Gemma was awake before dawn. She'd spent a restless first night in her new home, and all she really wanted was to close the shades and sleep all day. Unfortunately, there was too much to do, and Opal to think of, so that wasn't an option. Gemma hoped her daughter had fared better sleeping in her own room.

Opal had stayed outside until well after dark, then just picked at the dinner Gemma had prepared. Gemma received little more than a grunt or two by way of conversation, and then Opal declared she was going to bed.

Recent interactions with her daughter gave her whiplash, and Gemma was constantly reminding herself not to overreact, not to take it personally. Opal was in pain, and it was Gemma's job as a mother to keep cool under pressure. Eventually Opal would come around, but until then, Gemma would simply hold out for those fleeting moments when her sweet girl resurfaced once again.

She spent an hour or so sitting at her window seat, staring out at the waves and watching the sun rise. Gemma decided she could get used to starting her mornings that way. Once the sun was fully risen, she figured it was time for her to do the same, so she threw on some clothes and went down to the kitchen. She wanted to make a decent breakfast and have it ready when Opal woke.

She made a pot of coffee, poached a few eggs, and popped two bagels into the toaster. Unlike most teenagers, Opal tended to be an early riser, so Gemma knew she would be down before long. As if on cue, the floorboards creaked above her head. After a few minutes, Opal stomped down the staircase, her Doc Martens thudding on each step.

Opal was dressed in her typical attire—black hoodie, torn-up jeans, and skull-covered Docs. She was also wearing the expression of a teenager who did not want to have a conversation with her mother. Taking a deep breath, Gemma decided to test the waters.

"Morning, sweetheart." She worked to make her

voice sound cheerful. "I made coffee and eggs. The bagels you like are just about ready to pop up."

"I'm not very hungry. I'll just take the bagel." Opal walked across the room and grabbed the bagel as it popped up, wrapping it in a paper towel.

"You don't want eggs? Or orange juice?" Gemma tried again.

"No. I'm going to go explore this town you've forced upon me," Opal announced.

"You don't know where you're going. How am I supposed to find you?" Gemma tried to keep the panic out of her voice.

"I promise to text you every hour and let you know I haven't been kidnapped. Will that make you feel better?" Opal's irritation was obvious.

"A little, I guess."

"Fine. See you later." Opal gave a half-hearted wave and headed out the front door.

Not satisfied with how the conversation had gone, Gemma followed her daughter onto the porch.

"Be careful, honey. Really. I know you think I'm overprotective, but I worry about you."

"You don't need to. I'm fifteen, not ten, Mom," Opal quipped with a roll of her eyes. "I'll be back later. I'll text you in exactly one hour."

Opal sprinted down the stairs, across the front

yard, and down the dirt driveway, giving Eric a wave as his truck rolled slowly past her toward the house.

Not sure what to do with herself, Gemma stood on the porch, hands on her hips, watching as her daughter disappeared into the distance.

"Good morning," Eric said as he climbed out of his truck. "Your girl is off to an early start."

Gemma sighed, willing her voice not to quiver. "Yeah, it seems she can't get away from me fast enough these days."

"Teenagers, right?" Eric gave her a sympathetic smile. "I don't think there's any amount of money I'd take to go back to that age."

"Me neither, I suppose. But let me tell you, raising a teenager is way harder than being one. It's like trying to interact with a feral cat. They're either going to claw your eyes out or run the other way."

Gemma slumped into her Grandma Emerald's rocking chair on the front porch.

"Well, moving at that age is hard. New school. New people. New house. New town. I'm sure she's leaving behind a lot of friends." Eric leaned against the front porch, smiling up at her while she rocked in the chair.

Gemma watched him for a moment. He was completely comfortable in his own skin. He had a sense of quiet calm that gave her the sensation of taking a very deep breath. She realized she'd been holding hers, so she exhaled, letting it out.

"That's true," she began. "Opal left behind everything familiar. I keep reminding myself of that. Not to mention the fact that she lost her father a year ago. It's been a big black hole of sadness and loss for her."

"And for you," Eric added, compassion filling his blue eyes.

"Yeah, for me too," Gemma agreed, brushing away the tears that suddenly began to trickle from her eyes. "But I'm an adult. I can handle it. I worry for my daughter."

"I'm sure that's the case. That's what moms do, right?" He smiled.

"According to my daughter, all I do is worry," she admitted.

"I have a feeling that girl of yours is going to come out of this okay. She has a strength about her that you don't see in a lot of teenagers. It just sort of radiates from her."

"Yeah, it does, doesn't it?"

"You have the same thing." Eric's eyes held hers for a moment too long.

"I don't feel very strong right now." Gemma

sighed, looking away quickly. She felt as if Eric Johnson could see too much.

"You're a warrior, Gemma. I see it all over you," Eric answered quietly, giving her a look she couldn't quite define.

"That may be one of the nicest things anyone has ever said to me."

Gemma was taken aback that Eric would notice something so personal when he barely knew her.

"I'm just honest." Eric shrugged. "People either like it or hate it."

"You're also very observant."

"I have to be in my line of work."

"Restoring old houses?"

He nodded. "Sure. Old houses hold on to the memories and feelings of things that happened inside their walls. When I go into a place, the first thing I do is observe and listen. The house always tells me what it wants."

"You are an unusual man, Eric." Gemma laughed. "And I mean that in the best possible way."

"Thanks." He grinned.

"I have a feeling my grandmother would have liked you a lot. She would be happy to have someone like you working on her house."

"Oh, Emerald and I have spoken many times," Eric answered.

"Really? I had no idea. I guess I chose the right guy for the job, then." She chuckled.

"Maybe the house chose."

"I never thought of it that way." Gemma stood and headed toward the door. "Are you hungry, Eric? I made breakfast, and Opal didn't want anything. I'd hate to see it go to waste."

"I'm always hungry," he replied, ducking slightly as he followed her inside.

Gesturing toward the old broom above the door, she asked, "You don't happen to know what the deal is with the brooms, do you? There's also one hanging above the door in the jelly closet."

"They're for protection," Eric explained.

"Really? That's strange," she scoffed.

"Perhaps." He smiled. "They're thought to sweep away negative energy."

Gemma shrugged as she poured Eric a mug of coffee, which he drank black, and then she handed him a plate with eggs and a bagel. She fixed one for herself and joined him at the small table in the breakfast nook.

"I think today would be a great day for you to teach me how to use those fireplaces. It makes the house feel so much cozier in the evenings. I know it's technically still summer, but last night, I could definitely feel fall creeping in," Gemma mused.

"I can do that. I'm also going to work on winterizing your windows today. Honestly, they all need to be replaced, but my advice is to wait until next summer for that. For now, we'll just put some weather stripping around them to keep the cold out," Eric said between bites.

"That sounds good to me."

"So, what do you do for work, Gemma?"

"Well, I've been a journalist for the past seventeen years, but I quit my job when we moved, so I guess I don't really have one now," she answered with a shrug.

"You're a writer, then? I can see that." He nodded, observing her closely.

"I've been tossing around the idea of writing a novel for several years, but it never seemed to be the right time. I was thinking maybe I could give it a shot now that I'm officially unemployed. I have a bit of money saved from the sale of our house in Seattle, and since I don't have to pay for a place to live, and Grandma Emerald took care of paying for home repairs, it seems as good a time as any."

"You should definitely write a book. You'll be very good at it."

"How could you possibly know that?" Gemma

laughed. "You just met me. I could be the world's worst writer."

"But you're not. And you'll write your novel," Eric predicted.

"For some reason, it sounds possible when you say it." She smiled. "You actually remind me a lot of my grandmother, oddly enough."

"Do I? How so?" he asked.

"I'm not exactly sure. But you both seem to have the uncanny ability to know things you have no reason to know." She laughed.

"Is that a good thing?"

"Well, it's a bit strange, actually. I always felt like she knew things about me that I never told her. You give me the same feeling."

Eric's forehead creased with concern. "I'm sorry if I make you uncomfortable. I sometimes have that effect on people. I've been told I can be a bit intense."

"Not at all. It's the complete opposite, in fact. I feel very comfortable with you, which makes no sense at all since you're basically a stranger.

"You know what they say—strangers are just friends you haven't met yet." He laughed.

"There's something so familiar about you."

"Maybe we knew each other in a former life." Eric grinned.

She shook her head. "I don't really believe in things like that."

"Well, Gemma, I suppose we'll sort it all out in time."

"Yes, I suppose we will."

Eric looked around the kitchen, then rested his hands on the table. "For now, how about I help you clean up this mess, and then we'll get to that fireplace lesson. How does that sound?" He grabbed both plates and headed toward the sink.

Gemma smiled. "That sounds like the best idea I've heard all morning."

Six

Opal was proud of herself for remembering the way into town. She had put on a brave face for her mother, telling her not to worry, but she'd actually been a bit concerned about getting lost between the house and the town proper. She hadn't, so that was a bonus.

Smiling, she shoved her hands into the pockets of her ripped jeans and strolled down Main Street. She would have never believed it, but Beacon Shores was actually kind of cute. It felt a bit like stepping back into time—very retro, in a cool way. Her dad had been a history teacher, and their love of the past was something they'd always shared. He would have loved the town. It was too bad he was dead. The man who loved history had become part of it.

Some days it seemed like her dad was just away on a trip or something, and Opal kept waiting for him to walk through the door and say, "Hey, kiddo," like he always did. One year later, she was still waiting. Her dad wasn't coming back. Sometimes the pain of that realization was so intense she thought it would swallow her up. In those moments, all she could do was lash out at whoever was closest, usually her mother.

Opal loved Gemma with a fierceness, and she always felt guilty when she was mean to her, but sometimes she couldn't help it. She knew none of it was her mom's fault, and Gemma was in pain herself. But that knowledge didn't seem to matter when the pain overtook her. She wanted someone to hurt as badly as she did.

Honestly, Opal didn't know what she would do without Gemma. She was the one constant in Opal's life. Maybe that was why she threw all the ugly feelings in her mom's direction—Gemma was her safe space. Opal knew she had her mom's love no matter what.

Taking a deep breath, Opal inhaled the salty scent of the sea. The coolest part about living in Beacon Shores, besides the fact that her Grandma Emerald's house was beautiful, was that the ocean was her backyard. She loved the water and always had. Maybe she would learn to surf or something now that she lived so close to it.

Strolling past the corner store, Opal stopped dead in her tracks. There was a boy, about her age, sitting on the front steps playing a guitar. She stood there, riveted in place, listening to the song he was singing. It was good. Really good. A singer and songwriter herself, Opal knew great music when she heard it, and the boy was playing something fantastic.

He must have felt her eyes on him, because he suddenly stopped playing and looked right at her. He pushed his hair—a bit long and shaggy, but utterly perfect in Opal's opinion—out of his eyes and smiled at her. She stared for a few seconds, then, realizing what she was doing, turned away quickly and started speed-walking in the opposite direction.

She didn't move fast enough, however, because she soon heard footsteps behind her.

"Hey, hey, slow down," he called.

Opal's cheeks burned with embarrassment. The last thing she wanted was to stop and talk to the boy, but having him chase her down the street was even worse. Sighing heavily, she stopped, smoothed her hair, fixed an uninterested look on her face, and turned around to look at him.

"Are you talking to me?" She kept her voice steady although her heart was racing.

"Yeah," he said, a bit winded. "You're a really fast walker."

"One of my many talents," she said sarcastically.

"I'm sure." He grinned, showing perfect teeth and dimples.

"Was there something you wanted? Or do you always chase girls down the street?"

Opal shoved her hands into her hoodie and tried to look calmer than she felt.

"You're new," he answered with a shrug.

"So?"

"I mean, I haven't seen you around before. I'm Ryder Davis. My family owns the store."

"Cool." She nodded. "I'm Opal Clayborn. My mom and I just moved here from Seattle."

"Seattle. Nice."

"Yeah, it is," Opal agreed a bit wistfully.

"Well, Beacon Shores is no Seattle, but it's all right."

"Sure." She rolled her eyes.

"What do you think of it so far?"

"We just got here yesterday, so I can't really say. I like the ocean, though."

"Where do you live?" Ryder asked.

"Moonstone House. Do you know it?" Opal replied.

"Oh yeah, everyone in town knows where that is."

"They do?"

"Yeah. It's a cool place. Most kids think it's creepy, but I've always liked it," Ryder said.

"Creepy? Why?"

"I don't know, really. Stories about things that happened there a long time ago." He shrugged.

"I don't know anything about that."

"The stories probably aren't true. You know, urban legends and stuff like that," Ryder added.

Opal shifted her weight, struggling to keep up the disinterested routine even as her heart raced.

"What grade are you in?" he asked.

"I'll be a sophomore. You?"

"Junior. But we'll probably see each other around school."

"Well, you'll be the one and only person I'll know, then." Opal rolled her eyes.

"It's a small school. Most people are cool."

"That song you were playing back there... I've never heard it before."

"That's because I wrote it."

"You wrote that? It's really good," Opal said.

"Thanks. Songwriting is kind of my thing. It's

what I want to do. Of course, my parents think I need to come up with a real job."

"Music can be a real job," Opal assured him.

"I know. My parents don't get it."

"I get it."

"Are you into music?" Ryder asked.

"Yeah, I've been playing the piano since I was a kid. I sing and write songs too," Opal admitted.

"Cool. Maybe we can jam together sometime."

"Yeah. Maybe."

Opal reminded herself not to come across as too excited.

"I'd like that a lot, actually." Ryder smiled.

"We'll see," Opal said noncommittally. "Anyhow, I'd better get going. It was nice to meet you."

"You too. And I meant what I said—I'd love to play music with you sometime."

"Maybe. See you around."

Opal turned and walked away quickly. Once she was sure he couldn't see her face, she let go of the smile she'd been holding back.

Beacon Shores might not be half bad after all.

Seven

Gemma was playing music on her phone while she organized the ingredients for dinner. She hummed along to the melody, light and content. She felt so much at home, as if she truly belonged at Moonstone House. There had been virtually no adjustment period; the house already felt like a part of her.

She placed the salmon filet into the baking pan and drizzled a little olive oil on top. She was concentrating on slicing lemons when Opal walked through the door. Gemma took a deep breath, bracing herself, uncertain which version of her daughter would enter the room.

"Hey, honey." Gemma smiled, continuing to slice the lemon.

"Hey, Mom," Opal replied.

Gemma breathed a sigh of relief, not detecting a single note of surliness. "How was your day? Did you do lots of exploring?"

She sprinkled salt and pepper on the salmon and finished it off by carefully arranging the lemon slices on top. Then she placed it on the counter next to the preheating oven and began tossing the salad.

"Yeah. It was okay. It was a long walk."

Opal opened the refrigerator and grabbed the container of orange juice. Pouring some into a glass, she downed the whole thing in a matter of seconds.

"What was the most interesting thing you saw?" Gemma wanted to coax more than a couple words out of her daughter. If she asked the right questions, that might actually happen.

Opal wrinkled her nose, appearing to contemplate her answer before saying, "Well, the town is really retro and cute. I sort of like it."

"It is something, isn't it? Beacon Shores is so quaint and interesting," Gemma replied. "It's like stepping back in time."

"Dad would have loved it here," Opal said wistfully.

"Oh yeah, he really would have. I can't believe we

never even visited. I always thought we would one day, but life just gets in the way, I suppose."

"Yeah, and then death gets in the way," Opal murmured.

"Yep. It certainly does." Gemma didn't have a better response, so she left it at that.

"So we're having salmon?" Opal said, swiftly changing the subject.

"Your favorite."

"Nice."

"Eric has some fishermen friends who gave him a bunch of it, and he shared a few pieces with us."

"Eric's cool. I saw him outside when I got home."

"He's winterizing our windows. It's going to get cold at night before long," Gemma said, grating some parmesan cheese on top of the salad.

"Is Eric staying for dinner?" Opal asked.

"No. Why would he be?" Gemma wrinkled her forehead in confusion.

"I don't know, Mom. The man gave us salmon. He's working outside. It seems polite to ask him to stay and eat some of it." Opal laughed.

"Do you think so?"

"Since when am I the one lecturing about manners? Of course I think so." Opal rolled her eyes at Gemma.

"You're right. Inviting him to stay would have been the polite thing to do. What was I thinking?"

"Clearly you weren't," Opal pointed out. "I'll make this easy for you. I'll go invite him."

"Good idea, honey," Gemma agreed, a bit taken aback.

Opal spun on her heel and went outside. Gemma watched in amazement. She couldn't believe how much Opal seemed to like Eric. Of course, he *was* extremely likable. Usually overly polite, Gemma was disappointed in herself for not thinking to invite him to stay when he gave her the fish.

Opal sauntered back into the kitchen, clearly pleased with herself. "It's settled. He'll stay."

"That's good." Gemma nodded.

"At first he said he didn't want to because he would be all messy after working, but I told him we don't care."

"It's nice to see my lessons about kindness have sunk in after all." Gemma laughed. "Sometimes I wonder."

Opal snorted. "Whatever, Mom. I'm always kind."

Gemma raised an eyebrow at her daughter.

"Well, almost always," Opal amended.

"Can you grab the salad dressing out of the refrigerator and set the table?" Gemma asked.

"Yep."

The two worked in companionable silence, and once her duties were performed, Opal said she wanted to go change her clothes. Glancing down at her sweats and beat-up T-shirt, Gemma decided she should probably do the same if it wasn't going to be just the two of them at dinner.

Sprinting up the stairs, Gemma went to her room. She fumbled through her closet, trying to decide what to put on. She had only a small portion of her wardrobe with her, and she didn't want to look like she cared too much about her appearance, because she didn't. Comfortable and casual best described her style. She thought it was just good manners to ditch the sweatpants, though.

Deciding on a pair of jeans and a long-sleeved cotton shirt, Gemma changed and headed back downstairs just as the oven timer buzzed. Grabbing a mitt, she pulled the baking dish from the oven and smiled as the aroma of salmon filled the kitchen.

"Opal, dinner is done," she called up the stairs.

"Coming," Opal said as she came down. "I'll go tell Eric the food's ready."

Gemma smiled to herself when she saw that Opal had changed out of her angry teenager uniform. She had put on jeans—without a single hole in sight—and a cute blue zip-up shirt she hadn't worn in ages.

"You look nice," Gemma declared. "Not a speck of black clothing anywhere."

"Whatever. Don't get used to it." Opal smirked.

"Oh, I know better than that." Gemma giggled.

Opal went outside, and a couple minutes later, Eric followed her into the kitchen.

"You can use the bathroom down the hall if you want to wash your hands or anything," Gemma offered.

"Thank you. Are you sure you won't be bothered by my dirty clothes?" Eric asked.

"We don't care about your clothes," Opal answered decisively.

"We're just glad you could join us," Gemma added.

"Thanks for the invitation," he said. "I'll be right back."

~

As Gemma and Opal took their seats at the table, Eric disappeared into the bathroom, joining them a couple minutes later. Gemma dished up the food, and they all dug in.

"This is delicious," Eric said between bites.

"It's really fresh. Thanks for bringing it to us," Gemma answered.

"How long have you lived in Beacon Shores?" Opal interjected.

"Since I was born. My family has been here for as long as anyone can seem to remember," Eric replied. "My parents passed away a few years ago in a car accident and left me their house, so I stuck around."

"I'm so sorry to hear about your parents," Gemma empathized.

"Thank you. Losing the people you love is never easy."

"Is your house close by?" Opal questioned.

"Just down the road, actually. It's called Whispering Winds Manor. It's the huge brick monster with the wrought iron gate." He laughed.

"It's so cool how all the old houses have names," Opal commented.

"We passed your home on the way here, Eric. It's gorgeous," Gemma told him.

"It is. It requires a lot of upkeep, but luckily, I'm pretty handy when it comes to fixing things." He chuckled.

"I'll bet you know some really cool stories about the town," Opal said.

"I do. There's a lot of history here. Did you know that Beacon Shores has burned twice?"

"Really? Like the whole town burned down?" Opal leaned in, clearly interested in what he had to say.

"Most of it. The fires were pretty devastating. The first one was in 1899. They rebuilt, and then another one happened in 1905," he divulged.

"Wow. That's really weird that the same town would burn down twice within just a few years," Opal said.

"There are a lot of stories about the reasons behind it, but we'll save those for another day." Eric smiled. "For now, we should enjoy this amazing dinner your mom made for us."

"Okay, but you'll tell me all the stories, right? Please? I love history," Opal pleaded.

"Of course I will. All in good time." Eric nodded, shoveling a bite of fish into his mouth.

He was glad Opal wanted to learn the history of Beacon Shores. That was important. She needed to understand the things that had happened and her family's role in them. But there was no rush. He didn't want to burden the Clayborn women with too much information too quickly. Knowing the whole story would only overwhelm them. They were both strong —that much was obvious—but they were also vulnerable. He felt fiercely protective of them, just as he knew he would.

Truth be told, part of his hesitation could probably be chalked up to self-preservation. No matter which way he tried to spin it, he was also trying to keep the lid on his own secrets. His story was unusual, and not everyone could handle it. The pieces had to be doled out in digestible chunks.

After all, if he came out and said, "I talk to dead people," no one would hear a single word he said after that. Eric needed the women to trust him. He needed them to listen to him. Their futures all depended on it.

Chewing the bite of salmon slowly, Eric glanced over Gemma's shoulder. What would she say if he told her that her grandmother was there at that very moment?

He met the old woman's green eyes, so much like those of her granddaughter and great-granddaughter.

"You'll protect them for me?" Emerald asked him.

Eric nodded, almost imperceptibly, and the old woman disappeared.

Eight

After breakfast the next morning, Opal announced that she was going to explore again.

"Where are you going?" Gemma asked.

"Out. I don't know. I'll be around." Opal shrugged.

Biting her tongue, Gemma decided not to argue. She had to learn to pick her battles. She tried to remind herself that her girl was growing up, and she needed to give her a bit of freedom, even though that was the very last thing she wanted to do.

"Fine. You can explore. But you have to text me regularly throughout the day, and if I text you and you don't answer, I'm sending out the search party."

"Whatever, Mom. I'll text you. I always do." Opal

gave Gemma a quick peck on the cheek and headed out the front door.

Once Opal was gone and Gemma had cleaned up the breakfast dishes, she stood at the counter contemplating how she was going to spend her day. Her furniture hadn't arrived, so she had no unpacking to do. She had already cleaned every room in the house, and she was caught up on all the laundry they had with them.

Sighing heavily, Gemma knew what was going on —she was procrastinating, and she'd done it long enough. One of the biggest benefits of coming to live at Moonstone House was that she could finally write her book. It was something she'd dreamed of doing all her life. The problem was she'd never imagined she would actually do it.

Writing a novel had always loomed somewhere in the future, a goal just slightly out of reach. The fact that it was out of reach made it seem somewhat achievable. It was easy to say she was going to do it when she had the time because she'd never had the time. Or maybe she'd just never made the time. Either way, now that she had nothing *but* time on her hands, writing a book seemed an insurmountable obstacle.

How did a person even go about crafting a novel? Gemma had no process, no direction. Sure, she'd spent her entire career as a journalist, but that was different.

She was always chasing a specific storyline, asking the necessary questions to get to the answers and then reporting her findings. Writing a book was different. It was creating something out of absolutely nothing. She didn't know where to start.

"You'll never know if you can do it if you don't try." A voice that was clearly her grandmother's echoed in the stillness of the room.

Gemma turned around in a circle, fully expecting to see Emerald standing there. Of course, she wasn't. Gemma was alone. But the voice had been so real.

Swallowing hard, she walked upstairs to her bedroom. She grabbed her laptop and flopped onto her stomach across the bed. Opening the computer, she created a new document. As she stared at the blank page and blinking cursor, Gemma sighed.

"I have no clue how to do this," she said aloud.

"Everything you need is right here, child," Emerald's voice responded.

Glancing around the room, Gemma shook her head. Grandma Emerald wasn't there, but the sound of her voice was clear.

"I guess this is what I'm doing now. Talking to my dead grandmother."

Gemma waited, half expecting an answer, but there was none.

Chewing on the skin around her nails, she tried to empty her brain. She thought about story possibilities. The ideas were endless. She could write about anything. But maybe that was the problem. There were too many options.

Closing her eyes, Gemma rested her head on her crossed arms, letting the thoughts wander and flow. She forced herself to relax, to slow her breathing. Before she knew it, she was drowsy and felt sleep creeping closer. Rather than fight it, she gave in, drifting off to the place where dreams awaited.

~

Gemma didn't know how long she'd been asleep, but she was suddenly startled awake by a sound she couldn't ignore. Blinking her eyes to clear them from sleep-fog, she sat up on the bed. Her heart hammered inside her chest as the strange sound made its way to her ears.

It was a young girl's voice singing a song. Goose bumps erupted on Gemma's skin as the tune floated throughout the room.

"Listen close and you'll find me,
Buried 'neath the Remembering Tree.
Tucked inside and nestled deep,

Buried 'neath the Remembering Tree.

Hearts of hatred, hearts of greed

Seek the treasure buried deep.

Only she who holds the key

Will unearth the secrets of the Remembering Tree."

Jumping off the bed, Gemma ran down the hallway, checking each room to find the person who was singing. Each space was eerily empty, but the sound continued. She raced down the staircase, frantically inspecting every room downstairs. The voice followed her, but the area was empty as well.

Glancing outside, she saw Eric working in the yard. He was alone. Surely he would have let her know if someone had come inside the house. She checked all the doors. They were locked. Feeling uneasy, Gemma went back upstairs to her room.

As suddenly as it started, the song stopped.

Taking a shuddering breath, she tried to rationalize the phenomenon, but try as she might, there was no making sense of it. She was alone in the house, so who had been singing?

Sinking back onto her bed, Gemma glanced at her computer screen. The document was no longer blank. There were words on the page—words she didn't remember typing.

Swallowing hard, she leaned toward the screen, reading what was written.

Robert is gone. His poor heart gave out, and he has exited this world, leaving us alone. We came to this place, so far away from our people, to escape, but it seems trouble has followed us. Perhaps it was the building of the house that did it. My Robert worked himself to the bone day and night for two solid years to give us a sturdy home.

"I would give you the world if I could, my Pearl girl." That's what he used to say to me. In the end, it was all too much.

All I have left are my daughters and our traditions. Robert and I must instill in them a sense of their heritage, even though we crossed the country to leave it behind. It is clear my girls are gifted, but that isn't a surprise since both Robert and I practiced. The traditions run deep in both the Muller and Ackermann families, so our daughters, a combination of both lines, will continue our work.

Ru and Amie are my life, and I must prepare them for the fact that the world will not look kindly upon them, as it has not looked kindly upon me. No matter—we shall prevail. We know things, and the people of this town crave our knowledge and abilities, whether or not they want to admit it. We will use our knowledge for good. They can't fault us for that.

Something is coming, though. I can't see it clearly, but I worry it may be too strong for us to face alone. Only time will tell.

Gemma let out the breath she'd been holding as she finished reading. Where had the words come from? Had she written them? She didn't remember doing it, but how else had they been typed into the document on her laptop?

Not sure what to do with it, she decided to save it. Clicking the Save As option, she named the file "Pearl" and closed the laptop with shaking hands. The room felt stale, the walls closing in a bit too tightly. She needed some fresh air.

Walking downstairs, she headed out the front door and dropped into the old chair on the front porch. The wood creaked as she rocked back and forth in an effort to calm her racing heart. She watched as several butterflies flitted through the front yard, darting from flower to flower. As she rocked, a large butterfly landed on her arm, its wings glittering in the sunlight. As quickly as it landed, it flew away.

Gemma turned her attention toward the large tree in front of the house, examining it closely for the first time. It was tall, well over thirty feet, its vibrant pink heart-shaped blossoms adding a splash of color to the front yard. The blossoms danced and swayed in the breeze, and she could have sworn that it whispered something to her.

Rising from the chair, she climbed down the front porch stairs and stood next to the tree. Placing her palms flat upon the bark, she looked at it closely. She noticed the trunk was divided close to the ground, giving it an interesting shape. There were strange spots up and down the length of the trunk that looked like plugs or pegs. High above, a few strands of red hair had been stuck into one of the pegs and blew in the wind. Gemma wondered what that was about. Looking up through the pink-blossomed canopy, she smiled at the gracefully arched branches and rounded crown of the tree.

"You are a beauty, aren't you?" she whispered to the tree. "I think you're just showing off."

In the back of her mind, the words to the song she'd heard earlier began to play on a loop.

"Listen close and you'll find me, buried 'neath the Remembering Tree."

The bright blossoms of the tree rustled in the wind as if in response. Her palms grew hot and began to vibrate on the trunk. Afraid, she pulled her hands away quickly.

Although the tree was undoubtedly beautiful, there was something strange and unsettling about it as well.

"Pretty, isn't it?"

Eric's voice caused Gemma to gasp, and she nearly jumped out of her skin.

"I'm sorry. I didn't mean to scare you," he apologized.

"Don't even worry about it. I'm especially jumpy today." Gemma laughed, stepping away from the tree and turning toward Eric.

"That tree is something else, isn't it?"

"It really is. It's sort of mesmerizing, actually."

"It's a very old tree," he explained.

"A redbud, right? I think that's what it's called."

"That's right. Also known as a Judas tree."

"Judas tree?" Gemma asked.

"Yeah, it's supposedly the same kind of tree that Judas hanged himself from after betraying Jesus," Eric answered.

"Really? That's interesting. And kind of dark," Gemma replied.

"I suppose so." He shrugged. "I've never really thought of it that way."

"What are those spots that look like they've been plugged with something? One of them looks like it has hair in it," Gemma inquired.

"It's actually a folk healing practice called 'pegging' or 'plugging,'" Eric replied.

"What is that?"

"There's a much more complex answer, but it's the idea of using trees for healing. The healer places an illness into the tree and plugs it. Sometimes they place something belonging to the sick person, like strands of hair, into the plug. Basically, the healer measures the sick person against the tree, bores a hole in it at their height, and once the person grows past the point in the tree, they're healed. On the flip side, it's also said that if the tree dies, the person dies."

"That's very strange. Did someone around here use this tree for that?"

"Yes."

"It's kind of creepy. Who would do that?" Gemma shuddered.

"Let's see. Your grandmother, for one. Her mother as well, from what I'm told, and most of her ancestors," Eric answered.

"My grandmother plugged people's illnesses into a tree? She actually thought that worked?" Gemma smirked.

"She did," Eric replied simply.

"Hmm. Well, does the tree always have flowers this time of year? I mean, it's nearly fall. Don't redbuds usually flower in the spring?"

"Not this one. It always looks like this."

"What do you mean?" Gemma wrinkled her forehead.

"I mean this particular tree is always in bloom. Always," Eric answered.

"Even in the winter?"

"Always," he repeated.

"I don't understand. How is that possible?"

"I've lived here my whole life, and I've never seen it any other way. I'm not sure how it's possible, but that's the way it is."

"That doesn't even make sense," Gemma argued.

"Everything at Moonstone House operates on its own unique schedule," Eric answered cryptically. "And everything here has a story."

"I'm coming to realize that," Gemma said quietly, pushing away the chill that crept down her spine.

Nine

While Gemma was trying to make sense of strange singing voices and unusual healing trees, Opal was spending the morning exploring the woods connected to their property. As much as she hadn't wanted to come to Beacon Shores, she had to admit the place had quickly cast a spell on her, especially the woods.

The foliage was dense and thick, and she had the sneaking suspicion that she could easily become lost if she wasn't careful. Mostly, though, the woods were magical. The moss-covered logs and trees dripping with lichen gave an otherworldly quality to the forest. She wouldn't have been surprised in the least to spot a faerie or troll wandering around.

Opal plopped down onto a fallen tree branch and dug through her bag to find her protein bar. Guzzling her water, she took a bite as she listened to the birds chirping in the canopy above. She jumped when she heard a twig snap behind her, then smiled when she realized it was just a small squirrel scurrying up a nearby tree trunk.

Finishing her snack, Opal stuffed the wrapper back into her bag and took another drink from her water bottle before continuing on. She stopped to take a photo of a butterfly with her phone. It wasn't the best camera, but she ended up with a decent shot.

Walking a bit farther into the woods, she spotted a footbridge. Picking up her pace a bit, she arrived at a large creek. The water rippled over rocks that had been worn smooth over time. The creek was large, and the quaint stone bridge spanned its width.

Feeling as if she had discovered a hidden gem, Opal wandered across the bridge, stopping in the middle to lean over the railing. She pulled out her phone again and snapped a few photos. The dappled sunlight through the trees was perfect, and she decided then and there that she would frame one of the pictures and hang it in her new bedroom.

She was so absorbed in her surroundings that she

didn't hear footsteps behind her, so when she spun around and saw a girl standing there, she instinctively let out a scream.

"Sorry," the girl whispered, her eyes wide with fear.

Embarrassed at her reaction but recovering quickly, Opal replied, "It's not a big deal. I just didn't hear you coming, and you surprised me."

"Sorry."

"No need to apologize. I'm sorry for screaming." Opal laughed nervously.

The girl didn't say anything, just simply stood there staring at Opal, wringing her hands together. She looked to be about the same age as Opal, but she was wearing a dress that seemed better suited to the previous century. In spite of the outdated garment, the girl was beautiful.

Clearing her throat uncomfortably, Opal tried again. "I'm Opal. What's your name?"

Eyes wide, the girl had the mannerisms of a scared rabbit. Before Opal could say anything else, the girl turned quickly and darted away through the woods.

"Hey, come back! I'm sorry I screamed," Opal called after her.

It was no use. The girl was gone, disappearing into the thick forest like she'd never been there at all.

"That was weird," Opal said out loud. "So much for making a friend around here."

At the thought of a friend, Opal decided she would wander back into Beacon Shores and see if she might accidentally run into Ryder Davis—not that she would ever admit she was hoping to. Knowing the walk into town would take longer than she preferred, she picked up the pace.

About a half hour later, she wandered into the town proper. Strolling casually down Main Street, Opal walked toward the corner store. Trying to appear nonchalant, she stole a glance at the front door. She had to remind herself to keep the smile from her face when she saw Ryder sitting on the stairs.

"Hey, it's you," he called.

"It's me." She shrugged, telling herself she didn't care that he'd noticed her.

"I was hoping I would see you again."

"Well, here I am."

"I was just working on a song." Ryder nodded toward the guitar lying across his lap. "Want to hear it?"

"Sure." She walked up the stairs and sat down next to him.

Smiling widely, he positioned his guitar and began

to play. Opal recognized the song after the first chord. It just so happened to be her favorite. Ryder began to sing, and his voice, warm and smooth as velvet, caused goose bumps to erupt on her skin.

By the time he got to the chorus, she couldn't help herself. She had to join in. Overlapping her voice with his, she filled in the harmonies, smiling at how well their tones blended. They finished the song together, and Opal had to admit it felt like magic. Musically, they were a perfect duo.

When he played the final chord, Ryder looked at her, his eyes wide with wonder. "That felt amazing. You're amazing. I mean, your voice and harmony just blended with mine. Was it just me, or was that, like, really special or something?"

"It was pretty great. It was like we'd rehearsed it. It all felt really natural," Opal admitted, a huge smile spreading across her face.

"We have to make this a regular thing. Like, for real, I mean. Do you want to?" Ryder asked, his eyes practically pleading.

"I think I might like that, actually," Opal replied, realizing she couldn't have wiped away her smile if she tried.

"Then it's settled. We'll work out the logistics and

stuff, but I mean, we have to do this. We have to play music together."

"Yeah, I think we do. That was too good not to."

"I meant to tell you the other day that I think you know my cousin," Ryder added. "I mean, just so you know I'm not some strange creep or anything."

"I don't think I know your cousin. I don't know anyone here."

"Yeah, you do. Eric? The guy working on your house?"

"Eric is your cousin? Oh wow. Yeah, I do know him. He's actually really cool," Opal said.

"He's the best. He's one of the only people I know who is really supportive of me wanting a career in music."

"I like him. He had dinner with us last night. I told him he needs to tell me all the stories and history of the town and stuff. I like that sort of thing."

"If anyone knows, it's Eric."

Opal felt her phone buzzing in her pocket and pulled it out. It was a text from her mom checking in to make sure she was okay. She texted back, ***I'm alive and well. Be home soon.***

"That was my mom. I need to head back. She worries," Opal explained.

"I know the feeling. My mom does too. How about if I walk you there?" Ryder suggested.

Opal's heart danced inside her chest. "Sure. That would be cool. I mean, if you want to."

"I want to. Really."

Ryder smiled, and Opal melted inside.

Ten

A few weeks later, Gemma was cleaning up the breakfast dishes, trying hard to push down the knee-jerk impulse of protectiveness when Opal told her she had plans for the day—plans that included a boy. Rather than try to dissuade her daughter from her activities, she decided she would simply focus on keeping her as safe as possible while she was gone.

"I'm glad you have plans, but I need you to remember to text me while you're out." Gemma tried to sound nonchalant, but she needed to convey the importance of safety.

"I always do, Mom. I don't know why you feel the need to say it every time." Opal rolled her eyes and gulped down her glass of orange juice.

"Because I'm your mom. Worrying is what I do. It's part of my DNA. I'm helpless when it comes to fretting about you." Gemma knew she was helicoptering, but she wasn't quite sure how to stop it.

"You know where I'll be—Ryder's house, which is next to the store. We'll be practicing music stuff. Eric already told you Ryder's a good guy and his parents are safe. Don't worry," Opal emphasized.

"Well, that's just not possible, honey." Gemma chuckled.

"I know it's not. I don't know why I bother saying it." Opal shook her head and smiled good-naturedly.

"Well, I do feel better knowing Eric has vouched for this young man. And I think it's wonderful that you're making friends and getting back into music. Really, I do."

"It is pretty great," Opal agreed.

"And I'll do my best not to worry, but you know how that goes."

"I know. I'll text you when I get into town and I'm with Ryder," Opal said.

Gemma pulled Opal close and hugged her tightly. She was happy Opal was getting used to the town and giving it a chance. It was what she had hoped for when they arrived. She couldn't believe the ways her daughter had changed already. The move had been good for her.

"Okay. Ryder's walking you home so you don't have to do it alone?" Gemma clarified.

"Yep. His family invited me to stay for dinner, and if it's dark when we're done eating, his mom said she would drive me home."

"I like that plan. It's a solid one." Gemma nodded, the knot in her stomach loosening a bit.

"Love you, Mom," Opal called as she darted out the front door.

"Love you too, baby," Gemma returned.

She had just finished the last of her coffee when Eric popped his head in the front door. "Hey, Gemma, can I come in?"

"Sure thing. I'm in the kitchen," she answered.

"Good morning." He smiled as he leaned against the countertop.

"Want some coffee?" Gemma asked, grabbing a mug and filling it to the top before he could even answer.

"You know I do."

He grabbed the mug and took a big gulp of the smooth black liquid.

Coffee and home renovation conversations had become their normal morning routine over the past few weeks. Sometimes Opal joined them, if she wasn't otherwise occupied with her blossoming social life.

Gemma had come to think of Eric as a friend and confidant. He had proven himself to be kind and self-less, always going above and beyond. He had even helped them move in all their furniture and belongings when the truck came the previous week. Gemma had to admit that she had grown quite fond of their morning chats.

"So, we're planning on repairing some of the floor-boards in the extra bedroom today, right?" Gemma rinsed out her mug and stacked it in the drain rack.

"Yep. It shouldn't take long, but it needs to be done. You don't have much in that room yet, so we should take care of the repair before you fill it up like you've done the rest of the place," he answered with a chuckle.

"Hey, believe it or not, I got rid of half of my stuff before we moved. You should have seen my last house." Gemma laughed.

"I can't even imagine," he joked.

"What can I say? I love home décor."

"Well, you have a definite flair for it. I can't believe how great this old place is starting to look." He glanced around the room and smiled in appreciation.

"I'm pretty sure most of that is your doing. You're the one giving it a facelift."

"But you're the one making everything beautiful. You have a knack for that too."

Gemma felt heat rush to her cheeks. "Maybe we should just agree that we make a good team."

Eric's eyes twinkled, and her stomach flipped.

"I won't argue with that," he said with a smile. "We're pretty good together."

Neither spoke for a full thirty seconds.

Just before the silence grew uncomfortable, Eric said, "Let's head upstairs. I'll bring the tools."

Gemma led the way to the spare bedroom. Eric dropped his tools onto the floor and walked to the far corner of the room. Crouching to his knees, he wiggled the damaged boards.

"There are about six boards here that we need to replace. They aren't completely compromised, but they're well on their way. It makes sense to take care of them now before they get worse."

"Sounds good to me. You know how this routine works. You tell me what to do, and I will be your dutiful apprentice." Gemma gave him a mock salute and a wide grin.

"You're the best apprentice I've ever had." He laughed.

"I highly doubt that," she replied with a roll of her eyes.

"Well, you are." He grinned. "You're also the only apprentice I've ever had."

"Ah, well, it all makes perfect sense to me now."

Gemma had never been one for home renovation, but Eric was extremely knowledgeable. He was also a great teacher, and he made it fun. She had learned how to do a lot of projects in the past couple weeks working side by side with him.

She watched as Eric grabbed a carpenter's square and drew a line across the section of wood he intended to remove.

"Can you hand me the power drill, please?" he asked.

"Sure thing," she answered, handing it to him.

Eric drilled some holes along the marks he had made, then grabbed a wood chisel and split the damaged beams into pieces. Then he removed the boards, prying them up one by one.

"I'm going to measure this now, and then we can go outside and cut some new boards," he explained, tossing the old wood aside.

He was just about to stand up when something caught Gemma's eye.

"Eric, what's that?" She pointed at an object nestled beneath the floorboards.

Eric leaned down, getting a closer look.

"It's a box," he replied, pulling it out of the hole and blowing a cloud of dust off the lid.

"Wonder what's inside?" Gemma asked, taking it from his hands.

"Let's take a look."

She gently lifted the lid. "Check this out."

Gemma showed him what was inside—three books. One was an old Bible. The second was a book with a title that appeared to be German, *Der Lange Verborgene Freund*. The last looked like a journal. She grabbed it, surprised when it seemed to pulse beneath her fingertips. Plopping down onto the floor, she opened it carefully, trying to steady her shaking hands.

"This is amazing," she said as she flipped gingerly through the time-worn pages. "The front cover has a name on it. It looks like it belonged to someone named Pearl Muller-Ackermann."

"Pearl, huh? Well, that's interesting," Eric replied.

"Yes it is. I wonder who Pearl might have been."

Gemma took a few shaky breaths, remembering the name Pearl from the strange words that were written on her computer.

"There's something else here. It looks like some

sort of inscription. It's written in another language—German, I think. But the English translation is there too," Gemma mused.

"What does it say?"

"*Herr Jesu dir leb ich, Herr Jesu dir steb ich, Herr Jesu dein bin ich todt un lebendig...,*" Gemma read awkwardly.

"What's the English translation for that?" Eric chuckled.

"Lord Jesus, I live to thee, Lord Jesus, I die to thee, Lord Jesus, I am thine, in death and in life."

"That's beautiful," he said quietly.

"It really is."

Eric sat down on the floor beside Gemma, peering over her shoulder at the journal.

"How much do you know about your family history, Gemma?"

"My family history? Basically nothing. Why?"

"Because living here, in this old house... I think it's going to be important for you to explore that. Having grown up here, I know a little bit about it, but why don't you fill me in on what you know first?" Eric urged.

"Well, my mother never talked about her family. She and Grandma Emerald had a falling-out when I was a kid, so other than a few letters we exchanged and spending summers with her until I was eight, I know virtually nothing about her. The only thing I know is that all the women in our family are named after jewels. I have no idea why."

"That's all you know?"

"Yep. That basically sums up my family knowledge. Pretty sad, huh?" Gemma shrugged.

"Knowing where you come from is important," Eric said. "Especially in your case. You have a very interesting family history."

"I've always wanted to know more. You said you knew things about my family, right?"

"I do. The woman who wrote this journal, Pearl, would have been your great-great-grandmother," he explained.

"Oh, wow. It's so cool that I have her journal." Gemma thumbed through the pages almost reverently. "The old Bible and that German book are great too."

"They're definitely hidden treasures," Eric agreed.

Flipping to the end of the journal, Gemma pointed to the page in front of her. It was a handwritten chart. She took a deep breath and read out loud.

Muller-Ackermann Braucheri:

Pearl, mother of Ruby and Amethyst

Crystal, daughter of Amethyst
Emerald, daughter of Crystal
Topaz, daughter of Emerald
Gemma, daughter of Topaz
Opal, daughter of Gemma

"It's a maternal family tree. *My* family tree," Gemma said quietly, cradling the book to her chest. "Grandma Emerald must have written this."

"This is a wonderful find. I had no idea they would be hidden here," Eric replied.

"But you knew my great-great grandmother's journal and the other books existed?"

"Emerald said they did. I started to believe they weren't real at all," he answered. "She hid them away before she went into the nursing home and then couldn't remember where she put them."

"Why would she hide them?"

"She was worried someone would find them. Someone who wouldn't understand."

"Understand what?"

"What she was. What the women in your family have always been," Eric said quietly.

"What does that mean?" Gemma asked.

"Your family is special, Gemma. Emerald wanted to protect that."

"I don't understand."

"The journal was written by Pearl, the woman who helped build this house. Your family is a bit of a legend around here," Eric explained.

"Legend? Why?"

"The women of Moonstone House are gifted, Gemma."

"Gifted? How?"

"Pearl and Robert, the ones who built this house, were both Braucherei healers. So were their descendants."

Gemma narrowed her eyes. "I have no idea what that means."

"I'm not surprised. It's kind of obscure, especially in this area of the country," Eric said.

"Can you explain?"

"Braucherei is a type of folk medicine of Pennsylvania Dutch origin."

"Pennsylvania Dutch? But this is Washington. How would something like that make its way out here?"

"I'm not completely certain, but I'm guessing it has to do with Pearl and Robert. Emerald told me that Pennsylvania was where they came from."

Gemma's eyes widened. "That's amazing. I mean, I always thought my grandma was sort of magical. I guess maybe she was."

"Well, the people of Beacon Shores have always been fascinated by this place, and by the women in your family."

"The townspeople will be sorely disappointed to learn that any and all magic ended at my generation." She chuckled. "There's nothing special about me."

"I'm going to have to disagree with you on that one. You're very special, Gemma. You just can't see it yet."

She shook her head. "I don't know, Eric. I'm just an average woman."

"You're anything but average. In time, you'll come to understand. It's in your blood."

Eleven

The next afternoon, Gemma and Eric worked side by side painting the large barn near the front of the property. They hadn't spoken again about Pearl's journal or the other books, but she had tucked them safely away in the top drawer of her dresser. She couldn't wait until she had time to sit down and look at the treasures. The comment Eric made about the women in her family having special abilities had gnawed at her since the discovery, and she hoped to learn more about it in the journal.

"Eric, what are these designs on the barn? They're beautiful and really intricate." Gemma gestured toward the circular signs depicting geometric shapes painted on the side of the barn they were working on.

"They're hex signs," he answered.

"Hex signs? Like a curse or something?"

"Not a curse. Just the opposite, in fact. Hex signs are common among the Pennsylvania Dutch, and all the symbols have different meanings. These are eight-pointed stars, which is sort of a proclamation of abundance and goodwill."

"That's so cool." Gemma smiled. "You're very smart, Eric. You're like a big bucket of obscure knowledge."

"Thanks. I love history and learning new things. Most people are bored listening to me ramble on about it."

"Not me. I was married to a history guy, remember? Feel free to astound me with your wisdom anytime." She laughed. "For instance, why is there a window painted next to the actual window on the barn?"

"It's a witch window," Eric replied, chuckling at the look of surprise on Gemma's face.

"You've got to be kidding me. What in the world is a witch window?"

"It's a painted replica of the actual window. The idea was that it would fool a witch who was trying to fly into the barn to ferhex the animals. Instead, she would crash into the false window."

"Ferhex?"

"Bewitch," he explained.

"Got it."

"There's also a SATOR square painted on the wall of the barn," he added.

"SATOR square?" Gemma raised her eyebrows in question. "I'm afraid I don't know what that is."

"Come with me."

Eric motioned for her to follow him inside the barn. There, painted on the wall next to the barn door, was a strange square configuration of letters.

SATOR
AREPO
TENET
OPERA
ROTAS

"And what might this be used for?" Gemma gestured toward the strange letters.

"For protection. It's a palindrome. It can be read from top to bottom, bottom to top, left to right, or right to left. It can be rotated 180 degrees and still be read the same way. It's been said to have magical properties. Supposedly the devil gets confused by repeating letters." Eric laughed.

"Wow. Your brain must be absolutely buzzing with information. If I had that much going on in mine, I think it would short-circuit, then crash and burn." She giggled.

Gemma took one last look at the letters and shivered slightly, a sudden cold chill creeping up her spine. Shaking her head to refocus, she followed Eric back outside, where they continued painting the barn.

She thought of all she had learned since coming to Moonstone House. Sure, she had always believed Grandma Emerald was a special woman, but didn't all little girls think that about their grandmothers? Eric said she was some sort of folk healer, but did Gemma really believe that? It seemed a bit far-fetched.

Of course, when Gemma really thought about it, Emerald had definitely been out of the ordinary. For instance, she always spoke to animals. What's more, they responded to her as if they totally understood, as if their conversations went both ways. Her grandmother could also make healing tinctures from things that grew from the land. Hadn't Gemma herself witnessed Emerald bringing plants back to life with nothing more than the touch of her hands and a few softly spoken words that sounded like some kind of gibberish? And her grandmother always knew what Gemma was thinking, often before she even thought it.

Gemma's own mother, Topaz, was a bit of a hippie, but hadn't she sworn she had dreams that foretold the future? Gemma chalked it up to her mother's eccentricity and overactive imagination, but the truth of the matter was that Topaz had known she had cancer and that she was going to die long before the doctor confirmed it. She had also told Gemma on more than one occasion when something big was going to happen. Invariably, Topaz had always been right. Had her mother been some sort of clairvoyant?

Was it possible that the women in her family possessed some not-quite-normal talents? Gemma thought about her own daughter's musical abilities. Sure, Gemma was a proud mother, but she had to admit that Opal's musical prowess was anything but average. At the age of four, Opal had sat down at the piano and composed a song without ever having had a lesson. Opal hadn't needed to be taught to play music. She simply knew how to do it.

Opal could pick up any instrument and play it like a master—without instruction. She looked at sheet music and read it on sight, no matter how complicated. But mostly, she played by ear, by feeling. Opal said the notes corresponded to colors and images in her mind. She had perfect pitch, and the voice of an angel. Opal was a musical prodigy, and there was nothing ordinary about that.

Gemma recalled a conversation where she asked Opal how she could play so many things so easily. At the time, Gemma passed it off as childhood imagination, but as she thought about it again, she remembered the details of the conversation more clearly.

"How can you play so many instruments, honey?" Gemma had asked. "You've never even had a lesson."

"The woman helps me by whispering into my ear. She tells me what to do," ten-year-old Opal explained.

"What do you mean, the woman whispers into your ear how to play music, Opal?"

"She tells me which notes to play. She sings into my ear, and I play what I hear."

"There's a woman who sings into your ear? What's her name?" Gemma had asked incredulously.

"Her name is Pearl."

Gemma shivered as she recalled the memory. Was it possible that the woman telling Opal how to play music was her great-great-great-grandmother Pearl?

Shaking the crazy thoughts from her mind, Gemma turned her head toward the sound of gravel crunching in the driveway. A strange car crawled to the end and came to a stop.

"Do you know who that is?" Gemma placed her paintbrush on the drop cloth.

"Not a clue." Eric frowned. "Want me to go with you to check it out?"

"Yes, please. I'm not expecting anyone."

The two walked side by side toward the car parked in the driveway, a fancy black Tesla. The driver door opened, and a man slid out. He was tall, with a commanding presence that was sure to make a person stop and take notice. His large frame was draped in a tailor-made suit, expertly hugging his well-maintained physique. He was clearly a man who understood his own charm and charisma. His slicked-back black hair reflected the sunlight, and his designer cologne wafted in the breeze, tickling Gemma's nostrils.

"Hello, folks. I hope I'm not interrupting."

The man smiled, flashing a perfect row of pearly white teeth. He casually slipped his mirrored sunglasses into the pocket of his suit jacket.

"What are you doing here?" Eric asked.

Gemma was surprised by the cool reception the always-friendly Eric gave the man. He didn't offer to shake the stranger's hand, but instead shoved his own hands into the pockets of his worn-out jeans. He stared, unsmiling, at the visitor.

"Eric Johnson, I haven't seen you in ages," the man said. "Not since we graduated."

"It's been a while," Eric said tersely.

"What are you doing here? This isn't your house, is it?"

"You know very well this isn't my house. I work here. I'm restoring Moonstone House," Eric replied, shifting his weight from one foot to the other.

"Imagine that. Small world, huh?"

"Too small."

The man turned toward Gemma. "Well, since my old pal Eric isn't going to introduce us, I'll take care of that myself. My name is Dominic Becker."

He extended his perfectly manicured hand. Not wanting to be rude, she shook it.

"Nice to meet you, Mr. Becker. I'm Gemma Clayborn, and Moonstone House belongs to me," she replied coolly.

"Well, aren't you a lucky woman? This place has quite a history attached to it," Dominic said, giving the house a sweeping glance.

"So I'm learning," Gemma answered. "What can we do for you, Mr. Becker?"

"Please, call me Dominic. Mr. Becker was my father." He chuckled.

"Very well. What brings you here, Dominic?"

"Business, actually. I'm a property developer, and I'm interested in buying yours."

She raised a brow. "You want to buy Moonstone House?"

"I do. I can promise you more than a fair price for it," Dominic said.

"That's very kind of you, but Moonstone House is not for sale," Gemma declared.

"I'm willing to pay well above market value. With the price I'm prepared to offer, you'll be a rich woman." Dominic flashed her a brilliant smile.

"It's not about the money. This property has been in my family for over a century. I intend to keep it that way. It will belong to my daughter someday," she said with a tight smile.

"That's all well and good, but think of the work and headache, not to mention the money you'll sink into this place to restore it," Dominic argued.

"I'm not afraid of a little work, Mr. Becker," Gemma said icily. "Besides, Eric is the best contractor around, and he's making everything quite easy for me."

"Yes, I imagine he is." Dominic raised his eyebrows and gave them both a smug look. "I'm sure it's quite cozy in there, the two of you together, working side by side on those long nights."

"I don't like what you're insinuating, Becker. Gemma is a respectable woman, not to mention my employer. If I ever hear of you saying one word that might suggest otherwise, you'll have me to deal with," Eric said tightly. "Now, it's time to get into your fancy car and make your way back to whatever rock you slithered out from under."

"I see I've touched upon a nerve. Very well, I'll be on my way. But I'm going to leave my card in case you change your mind."

Dominic reached into his suit pocket and pulled out a business card. He placed it into Gemma's trembling palm and gave her a long, lingering look. His fingers brushed her hand, remaining far longer than she would have liked. The darkness behind his eyes made her blood run cold. Taking an involuntary step away from him, she shoved the business card into her pocket.

She was about to speak when a woman's voice whispered into her ear, *"Cross of Christ and Crown of Christ and Jesus Christ; red blood, be to me at all times and all hours good. God the Father is before me. God the Son is at my side. God the Holy Ghost is behind me.*

Who now is stronger than these three persons may come to seize me?"

She glanced back and forth from Eric to Dominic, but neither man seemed to have noticed the voice.

"Did you hear that?" Gemma asked, her forehead wrinkling with confusion.

"Hear what?"

"The, uh, er...," she faltered.

"Are you okay, Gemma? You're white as a ghost."

"I-I don't know. I feel... strange. Cold." She shivered, wrapping her arms around herself for warmth.

"It's time for you to go now, Becker." Eric put a protective arm around Gemma's shoulders and glared at Dominic.

"I'll see you two around. Remember, Gemma, I can make you rich and take this old place off your hands," Dominic said, then slid back into his car and drove away slowly.

"Well, that guy hasn't changed a bit," Eric said disdainfully as he watched Dominic's car back down the driveway. "He's still the same pompous jerk he was when we were kids."

"I didn't like him at all. There's something really dark about him. He gave me the creeps." Gemma shivered again.

"Are you okay? You looked like you might pass out for a second."

"I'm good now that he's gone. There was this eerie blackness that sort of hung above him like a cloud. I've never experienced anything like that before." She chose not to tell Eric about the strange words she had heard.

"There's not much to like about Dominic, or any of the Beckers for that matter."

"Well, I'm glad he's gone. If I never see him again, it'll be too soon," Gemma replied. "What do you know about him?"

"Too much," Eric stated matter-of-factly. "We went to school together, and he was a world-class scumbag even back then. It seems like not much has changed. His family has money. A lot of it. They develop land. The Beckers lived in Beacon Shores for generations, but several years ago, Dominic's father died, and Dominic moved the business to the Seattle area. He still has a house here, and he comes back every now and then."

"I wonder what he wants with Moonstone House."

"He wants to buy it up, parcel it off in small lots, and make a ton of money. He doesn't care about preserving history. He wants to destroy it. He wants control."

The muscles in Eric's jaw tightened. He was angry, and Gemma was intrigued to see this side of him. The way he had jumped to her defense was sweet, and it made her feel protected, something she hadn't felt in a long time.

"Well, I'm glad he's gone. What do you say we finish painting the barn, and then you can stay for dinner?" Gemma suggested. "I have a new pasta recipe I've been wanting to try, and Opal won't be around. I honestly don't want to be alone tonight."

"That sounds like a plan to me. I'll help you cook."

"Thanks, Eric. Like I said earlier, we make a good team," she said with a smile.

TWELVE

Opal: Be there soon. Making a stop first.

Ryder: Hurry. Want to work on that song.

Opal: Calm down. I'll be quick.

Opal smiled and dropped her cell phone into her pocket. She and Ryder were practically joined at the hip. They had been hanging out for several months, and they texted nonstop. They also saw each other every day at school and worked on music most evenings. Being with him had really helped her during her first months at the new school. Because of him, she was no longer the new girl—she was Ryder's girl. Everyone loved him, which made Opal cool by association.

The couple always practiced music on Saturday

mornings, but Opal wanted to make a pit stop in the woods first. She'd been hoping to go back to the stone bridge ever since she'd seen it the first time. The photos she'd taken there were amazing, and she wanted to add to her collection.

Picking up the pace, she trekked deeper into the forest. It was so quiet and peaceful. She would have loved to spend more time there, but she'd promised Ryder they would practice, and she didn't want to let him down. Plus, she was excited to see him. It seemed she couldn't get enough of Ryder Davis.

Arriving at the stone bridge, she walked to the center and leaned over the edge. The sun-dappled water glistened and glimmered, and Opal knew it would make a cool photo. Snapping a couple shots, she lost herself for a few moments. Dropping her phone back into her pocket, she closed her eyes and drank in the serenity of the woods.

Her phone vibrated in her pocket, and she grabbed it again.

Ryder: Miss you.

Opal: You're pathetic. LOL. Miss you too.

Laughing to herself, she had to admit that she felt happy for the first time in a very long time. Things were changing for the better in her life, and as much as she hadn't wanted to come to Beacon Shores, she was glad her mother had the crazy idea to bring them to the little town.

Opal was focused on texting Ryder and wasn't paying close enough attention to her surroundings. That was why she hadn't noticed the group of guys standing at the end of the bridge until she was next to them.

"Look who's here. It's Ryder's little girlfriend," one of the boys sneered.

"Hey, baby, why are you wasting your time with that dude? You should be with someone like me," another added, smiling devilishly.

"Yeah, what's Ryder have that we don't? A guitar?" the third chimed in, laughing at his own lame attempt at humor.

Opal quickly shoved her phone into her pocket, took a deep breath, and tried to stay calm. She had seen the guys around school, but they didn't run in the same circles as Ryder and his friends. They hung out on the fringes, making trouble in class, and had a reputation for being the ones you didn't want to cross.

"Look, I don't want any trouble with you guys. I'm leaving now." Opal kept her head down and tried to move around them quickly.

The largest of the three stepped in front of her, blocking her path. The other two flanked her on either side.

"Not so fast, baby. Let's have a little fun first. What do you say, guys?" the big one taunted.

"Sounds good to me."

"She looks like she'd be a lot of fun."

Opal's heart beat quickly, and she wiped her sweaty palms on her pants. She knew if she reached for her phone, they would take it from her. If she ran, they would follow. They were bigger, stronger, and there were three of them. She was outnumbered and trapped.

Looking around frantically, she tried to make some sort of escape plan while reminding her heart not to beat out of her chest.

"It's not safe to be in the woods alone. Didn't your mommy ever tell you that?" one of the boys taunted.

"It's pretty secluded out here," another added.

"Yeah. No one will hear you scream." The third laughed.

The largest boy reached out to grab Opal by the shoulders, but just before he touched her, a girl's voice yelled, "Leave her alone!"

Opal whipped her head around quickly and saw the same girl from the last time she was in the woods—

the one who ran away. This time, the girl was standing in the middle of the bridge, and she didn't look like she had any intention of leaving. Instead, she pulled herself up to her full height and fixed an angry gaze on the boys.

The girl was small, and there was no way she could take on the guys alone, but there was a fierceness and intensity about her that Opal hadn't noticed the first time.

"It's her!" the largest boy said, his voice trembling.

"Let's get out of here," the other added.

"Run!" the third said.

Without another glance at Opal, the three boys ran through the woods, leaving Opal and the stranger far behind in a matter of seconds. Exhaling sharply, Opal wiped the sweat beads from her upper lip and tried to gain control of her racing heart.

"Are you okay?" the girl called from the bridge.

"I am now. Thanks to you," Opal replied, walking toward her on legs that felt like Jell-O.

"Those boys are terrible, but I've bested them before." She chuckled softly. "They know to leave me alone."

The girl smiled shyly, her small hands fluttering about, looking for a place to land.

"I'm Opal. And I'm pretty sure you just saved me from being attacked, so thank you."

"My pleasure."

"Do you have a name?" Opal smiled encouragingly.

"Ruby. My name is Ruby."

Opal observed the girl. She was very pretty, with shocking green eyes and wild, curly red hair. Her pale face was smattered with freckles. Opal imagined she'd been named Ruby because of her scarlet hair. She looked to be around Opal's age, but she seemed much older, mature, like she'd seen more than someone her age should.

Opal noticed that Ruby was wearing the same dress as before, one that was very outdated. Her shoes—black lace-up boots with small heels—looked as if they had seen plenty of wear. Retro clothing was very much in style, but this girl was taking it to another level.

"It's nice to meet you. Thanks again for saving me," Opal replied, not sure what else to say.

Ruby shifted her weight from foot to foot and looked around uncomfortably. She hadn't moved from the center of the bridge. Her eyes darted about quickly, and Opal had the feeling she was going to take off again.

Not wanting the girl to leave, Opal tried to make conversation. "Do you live around here?"

"Not far."

"Maybe you can come over sometime? I just moved here, and I don't have a ton of friends yet," Opal offered.

"I don't think so." Ruby shook her head slowly. "That wouldn't be a good idea."

"Oh, okay," Opal answered, confusion causing her forehead to wrinkle.

"I have something for you," Ruby said. "I've been thinking about giving it to you since I saw you in the woods the last time."

"You have something for me?"

"Yes."

"Can I see it?" Opal smiled.

Ruby reached into the pocket of her dress and pulled out a small pouch tied to a long piece of twine. She plopped it into Opal's outstretched hand.

"Wow. This is really thoughtful of you."

"It's important that you wear it," Ruby explained, her sharp green eyes flashing with intensity.

"Wear it? What is it?"

"It's to protect you," Ruby answered quietly.

"From the guys you chased off?"

"Them. And other things."

Opal placed the small pouch under her nose and sniffed it. “It smells like lavender. And what’s this little medal tied to it?”

“It’s filled with lavender, patchouli, and Solomon’s seal root. And that’s a St. Benedict medal. Inside is a Letter of Protection.”

“It’s amazing. I’ve never seen anything like it.”

“I don’t imagine you have. It’s mine, but I want you to have it. You must wear it always. Keep it next to you, touching your skin,” Ruby added.

“You said there’s some sort of letter inside? What does it say?”

“It says, *‘By the blood of Jesus Christ, the bearer of this letter is protected against all witchcraft, harm, disease, famine, sword, gunshot, poison, and death. In the name of God the Father and the Son and the Holy Ghost.’*” Ruby recited the words quickly, crossing herself three times when she finished.

“That was a whole lot of words.” Opal chuckled. “It sounds kind of old-fashioned. Like, from the Bible or something.”

“Yes.”

“Thank you. I won’t take it off,” Opal promised. “Hey, how old are you? What grade are you in? Do you go to our school?”

“I, uh... well, I-I have to go.”

Gathering her long skirt in her small hands, Ruby turned quickly and ran off the other side of the bridge, disappearing so fast that Opal second-guessed her having been there at all.

"Why does she keep running off like that?"

Sighing deeply, she slipped the strange talisman over her head, securing it beneath her shirt.

Ruby was gone, leaving Opal alone in the woods once again. Still shaken from the incident with the boys, she decided it was time for her to get out of there. She walked quickly toward the clearing, glancing around and listening for the telltale sounds of them returning. When she reached the edge of the woods, she took off running toward town.

It would be a while before Opal felt comfortable enough to return to the woods alone. The thought made her both angry and sad.

Thirteen

Opal was gone for the day, practicing music with Ryder, and Gemma felt restless and unmoored. She was supposed to be spending the morning writing, but so far, her attempts had been futile. She pulled up the file containing the strange words she still didn't remember writing. How had they made it onto her computer screen? If she hadn't written them, who had? Gemma read over them so many times she practically had them memorized.

After everything she had learned, she was beginning to believe that Pearl herself had somehow written the words from beyond the grave. The fact that she almost thought that could be true was enough to make Gemma fear she might be losing touch with reality.

"Pull yourself together. Ghosts don't type on computers," she whispered.

Glancing out her bedroom window, she saw Eric repairing the greenhouse in the front yard. Grandma Emerald had practically lived in that greenhouse, and at one time, it was a wonder to behold. Emerald had packed the space with every herb imaginable, as well as plants and flowers she used in her homemade tinctures.

Gemma had never had much of a green thumb, but since she'd come to Moonstone House, she felt compelled to grow things. Eric assured her he would help her learn, and he was determined to restore the greenhouse to its former glory.

Gemma offered to help, but Eric turned her down. Instead, he insisted she go upstairs and work on her book for a little while. How easy it sounded when he said it! He had so much faith in the idea that she could actually write a book. If only she could sit down and have the words just pour out of her. Sadly, they refused to come. The truth of the matter was that Gemma still had no clue what her book was even about.

If she were being honest, the only words in the file were ones she couldn't remember writing.

"Maybe I just need a little inspiration," she mused.

Walking to her dresser, Gemma opened the drawer and pulled out Pearl's journal. Carrying it to her bed, she flopped across the mattress and opened the book. She read some of the first pages, mainly passages about Pearl's daughters. They were the words of a young mother, and Gemma felt the pride and fear in Pearl's words when she spoke of her girls. Gemma knew that feeling so well. Motherly worry was something that transcended both time and space.

The journal was quite long and detailed. Flipping several pages ahead, Gemma stumbled upon words that grabbed her attention. Focusing on Pearl's old-fashioned script handwriting, she read the passage.

A woman from Beacon Shores came to Moonstone House today. Word has gotten out that I'm a healer. The woman has come to me asking for help. I told her I'm not a doctor, and I am not a magician. As a Braucherin, I'm simply an instrument of God. I also had to make sure the woman believed in God; otherwise, seeking my help would do her little good. God, not me, is the source of all healing.

The woman agreed and told me she had been sick for months. She didn't know what was wrong, and the doctors had been unable to help her. I decided that a charm for general sickness would be the place to start, so I asked her to come to me that evening, as it was the full moon. Once she arrived, I seated her in the chair and placed my Bible in her lap. Then I swept my hands over her body.

I measured a red string from the top of her head to the tip of her toes. I then used the string to measure the circle of her head and tied a knot, followed by measuring the circle of her chest and tying another knot. After that, I measured the length of her left arm and tied a knot. All of this was done while whispering the Lord's Prayer three times. Once I was finished, I burned the string. I told her to go home and that she would most likely be better by the morning.

The woman looked as if she wanted to ask questions, but she didn't. She seemed confused by my ways but assured me she believed. I am only here to help people. Time alone will tell if her healing is the will of God.

Gemma stopped and exhaled. What had she just read? Was it possible that Pearl truly believed she could heal people with her strange folk remedies? Measuring and cutting strings? Did other people believe that as well?

Flipping ahead a couple pages, Gemma scoured to see if Pearl had written about whether or not the woman had gotten well. Shaking her head in disbelief, she zeroed in on the words.

The woman came back to me the week after I burned the string. She brought me a cake she had baked as a thank-you gift for helping her. She said she felt better than she had in years, and she told me she knew it was because of what I had done for her. Thanks be to God.

"Pearl helped the woman. That string thing she did actually worked," Gemma said quietly. "How is that even possible?"

Deciding she needed to read more, she flipped ahead toward the middle of the journal.

Sterling has been at Moonstone House for more than a month now. He is a wonderful man, always helping me with chores and jobs that I don't seem to have time to get to. When he showed up that night, so ill he could barely walk, I knew I had to take him in. I had to help him. When he offered to stay on in the barn once he was well, to assist with chores, for some reason, I couldn't refuse.

His kindness speaks volumes, and although I don't know how long he'll be with us, I have a hard time thinking about what this place will be like once he's gone. I feel drawn to Sterling, and then guilty about that fact. I know Robert would wish me happiness, but am I brave enough to claim it? Robert has been dead for over a year, and I will admit that I'm lonely. I love my daughters, but sometimes I long for deep conversations with another adult.

Sterling has a way about him that I don't really understand. I feel myself come alive when he walks into the room. There is some sort of magic about him, and while I know he isn't like me, I believe he has some special gifts of his own. In time, I hope to uncover what they are.

Gemma stopped reading, realizing she was holding her breath. Letting it out, she reread the words. Pearl's feelings about Sterling struck a chord with her in a way that few things had. She couldn't help but draw a parallel between Pearl's situation and her own. Pearl had lost her husband, and she felt herself drawn to another man but experienced guilt about that attraction.

If she were being honest, Gemma understood that Pearl's words hit home because it was much the same thing that was happening to her in regards to Eric. When Pearl said she felt herself come alive when Sterling entered the room, Gemma could fully relate, because she felt that way with Eric. She knew she lit up like a light bulb when she was near him. It was the craziest thing.

But, like Pearl, she experienced the guilt that came from believing she was betraying her dead husband. Even though Clayton would want her to move on and be happy, Gemma felt guilty. It was crushing at times.

Ruminating on the words in the journal, Gemma couldn't help but notice that, although Pearl's words were written over a hundred years ago, the two women had much in common. Their lives had taken similar turns. They had shared the same experiences. She needed to know how Pearl's life turned out, thinking it might direct her on her own path. Had Pearl found happiness in the end? More than anything, Gemma wanted to believe she had.

Although Gemma wanted to find out immediately, there were other things she needed to do. Her own life was calling, and she must get back to it. Placing the journal in the top drawer of her dresser, she joined Eric outside at the greenhouse.

FOURTEEN

Gemma and Eric spent the rest of the afternoon working on the greenhouse. She couldn't believe the progress they had made on it by the end of the day.

"It looks amazing!" she exclaimed, clapping her hands gleefully. "Thank you for helping me do this."

"We did good work. We'll be ready for planting in the next couple days. We can go to the store and find the herbs and plants you want to grow." He smiled.

"I said I want to grow things, Eric. That doesn't mean I know what I want to grow." Gemma chuckled. "I told you, I know nothing about this."

"I know. And I told you I would help you, didn't I?"

"You did. You do that a lot, actually," she replied.

"What's that?"

"Help me. You've been doing it since I got here. And I just want you to know I appreciate it more than you can even imagine. I don't know how I would have done any of this without you. These last months, well, you've just helped me so much."

"It's been my pleasure, Gemma. Really."

Eric's eyes met hers and locked in place. Neither spoke for several seconds. She couldn't look away, but instead of feeling awkward, it almost seemed like they were having a conversation without words. The look conveyed things neither of them was ready to speak aloud.

Gemma jumped when the alarm on her phone went off. "Oops! Sorry for the obnoxiously loud sound. That's my signal to go get Opal."

"I'm assuming she's with Ryder? Those two seem joined at the hip these days." Eric laughed.

"They do. And yes, she's practicing music with him. I told her I would pick her up so she didn't have to walk. I get nervous about her walking home after dark, even if she's with Ryder."

"Well, I'm just going to work on a few more things around here, and then I'll head out for the night," he said as he tossed his hammer into his toolbox.

"Are we finishing up the greenhouse tomorrow?"

"If you want to help. I was actually hoping you'd be working on your book. How's that coming, by the way?" Eric leaned against his truck and stuffed his hands into the pockets of his jeans.

"Honestly? It's not really coming at all. I mostly just sit there and stare at the screen. Or else I open Pearl's journal and read that instead." Gemma sighed.

"Give it time. It'll come. I know it will. Just don't push it. If you try too hard, you'll only block yourself."

"You sound like you're speaking from experience." She smiled.

"I am, actually. I write poetry." Eric shrugged.

"Of course you write poetry." Gemma rolled her eyes and chuckled.

"Hey, what's that mean?" He smiled good-naturedly. "Are you making fun of me?"

"Not at all. Just the opposite, in fact. I mean, you're basically the perfect guy, so why wouldn't you write poetry?" She shook her head as her smile widened.

"Perfect guy? Hey, I like the sound of that." Eric laughed.

"Don't let it go to your head. Modesty is one of your best qualities." Gemma grinned. "Anyhow, I have to go. I'll see you tomorrow?"

"Definitely tomorrow. Have a good night,

Gemma." He held her gaze for a second, then went back to putting away his tools.

She slid into the driver seat of her vehicle, started it up, and drove into town. It only took a few minutes by car, but Gemma always got nervous when Opal walked home after dark. She drove down Main Street, pulled into a parking spot in front of the general store, and turned off the ignition.

Opal said that she and Ryder usually hung out in front of the store, but Gemma didn't see them. She grabbed her purse and went inside. She'd been in the store only once before, so she took her time and browsed through the aisles for a few minutes.

"Hello, there," a voice behind her said.

Turning around quickly, Gemma smiled at the woman. She was about Gemma's age but much taller. She was very pretty, with light blonde hair and blue eyes that looked like the ocean. Her smile was warm and friendly, instantly putting Gemma at ease.

"Hi," Gemma answered.

"You must be Gemma, Opal's mom? I think I would have known you anywhere. Your sweet daughter is the spitting image of you." The woman chuckled.

"Yes, it's true. We get that a lot. Opal hates it, but it's just a fact, I suppose. No getting away from genetics."

"Isn't that the truth? I'm Abigail, Ryder's mom. And as far as genetics go, I may have carried that boy inside my body, but his genes are all from his father's side."

Abigail laughed, and Gemma thought it sounded like music.

"It's so nice to finally meet you. Our kids seem quite taken with each other," Gemma replied.

"Oh, they do for sure. And we just love Opal. You've done a great job with that girl of yours," Abigail remarked.

"Ryder is great too. I haven't gotten to know him all that well, but Opal speaks quite highly of him, and her opinion of people is usually pretty accurate."

"Well, it's great to finally meet you in person. I mean, I've been hearing so much about you that I feel like I know you already," Abigail added.

"You've heard a lot about me? You mean from Opal?" Gemma wrinkled her forehead in confusion, surprised that Opal would have said much about her.

"No, from my cousin. I swear that man has talked about nothing else since you came to town. It's always 'Gemma this' or 'Gemma that.'"

"Your cousin? I'm sorry. I'm a little confused," Gemma explained.

"Eric. You know, the super-cute handyman who spends all his time fixing your house?" Abigail laughed.

Gemma nodded. "Eric. Of course. I mean, I knew he was your cousin, but I guess I sort of forgot about it."

"And speaking of being taken with someone, I would say that Eric is very taken with you." Abigail grinned.

"Oh, well... I, uh... I mean, Eric's great. Really great. But we're just, uh, friends," Gemma stammered.

"Don't worry, I know you're just friends. *Right now*. But let me tell you, I don't think I've ever seen him this chatty about a woman before. He literally talks about you all the time. He thinks you're the best thing since sliced bread," Abigail shared.

"Wow. Yeah, I mean... he's a great friend. A really good... friend." Gemma struggled to find words.

"Eric would absolutely kill me if he knew I said anything to you, so let's keep this between us girls, shall we?" Abigail laughed heartily. "And now I've gone and embarrassed you. I'm so sorry. Sometimes I just get excited about things and get ahead of myself. It's one of my worst qualities."

"No, it's totally fine. I won't say anything to him. Really," Gemma assured the woman.

Abigail continued asking questions about how

Gemma liked living in Beacon Shores and how the work on Moonstone House was going. Gemma did her best to keep up with the conversation, but her mind was racing a thousand miles a minute.

She had been struggling with her own attraction to Eric, but now that she knew for sure the attraction was mutual, what was she supposed to do with that information? Gemma wasn't ready for a relationship, but she also had to admit that when the time came for her to be ready, Eric was exactly the kind of man she would want.

"Hey, Mom, sorry I wasn't out front. We were playing our song for Ryder's dad," Opal said.

Gemma looked up and saw Opal standing there and realized she had completely missed the end of the conversation with Abigail. Ryder, Opal, and Abigail all stared at her, waiting for her to respond to something.

"Hmm? What did you say? I'm sorry, Abigail. I think I sort of zoned out for a minute or something. I guess I've been working too hard," Gemma offered, trying to explain her lack of response.

"Not a problem at all, honey. I was just saying that I'd love for you and Opal to come to dinner sometime next week if you're able to," Abigail replied.

"We'd love that. Or better yet, maybe you would like to come to Moonstone House for dinner? I haven't really had the chance to show off the improvements to anyone besides Opal and Eric," Gemma offered.

"That sounds like a plan. You just let us know when and what we can bring, and we'll be there," Abigail agreed. "My husband won't be able to make it because he'll be out of town, but Ryder and I can come."

"Perfect. It was so great to meet you, Abigail," Gemma added.

"See you tomorrow, Ryder," Opal said. "And thanks for having me over, Mrs. Davis."

"Anytime, sweetie," Abigail answered.

Gemma and Opal waved goodbye and headed to the car. As they drove toward home, Opal talked nonstop about the song she and Ryder were working on. Gemma nodded along and pretended to follow the conversation, but she was really thinking about what Abigail said in regards to Eric. Now that she knew Eric was attracted to her, would it make things awkward between them? She valued him as a friend, so she hoped not.

Just when she thought things were finally coming together, life had once again thrown her a curveball.

FIFTEEN

The next day, Gemma and Eric were working on the greenhouse again. It was so close to being finished, and Gemma couldn't wait to begin planting. She'd done some research the night before since she'd been unable to sleep and started a list of herbs and plants to grow. She was trying to keep her mind on the task at hand, but she was failing miserably.

She'd worked hard all day to act normal around Eric, which was far easier said than done. Now that she knew Eric was interested in her, and she felt the same way about him, convincing herself they should just stay friends was becoming increasingly difficult.

"Hello? Earth to Gemma... are you okay?"

Eric's voice made its way into her muddled thoughts.

"What? Er, sorry, did you say something?" Gemma's cheeks burned as she looked at Eric, who was shaking his head and smiling that lopsided grin in her direction.

"I asked if you could hand me the shovel. It's right there beside you. I said it three times, but I think you were somewhere else." He chuckled.

"Yeah, I guess I was," she replied. "Here you go."

She placed the shovel into his hands and tried not to look at him too closely, afraid he would be able to read her thoughts.

"Are you okay? You seem a bit off today," Eric asked.

"I'm fine. I just haven't been sleeping all that well lately," she deflected. "I guess it's finally catching up with me."

She went back to staining the piece of wood she'd been working on, hoping he would leave it at that. She should have known better, however. Eric was far too intuitive not to notice her introspective mood.

"Why haven't you been sleeping well? When I don't sleep well, it's usually because I'm worried about something. Is there anything you'd like to talk about? We're friends, Gemma," he offered gently.

"Friends." She sighed. "Yes we are."

"So, are you going to tell me what's bothering you? Or are you going to make me guess?"

"It's nothing, really," she lied.

"Gemma...."

Eric propped the shovel against the side of the greenhouse, grabbed her by the hand, and led her outside to the nearby picnic table. He straddled the bench, and she sat facing him. He was close enough to touch, but she shoved her hands into her pockets, tried to close herself off, and pushed down the swarm of butterflies in her stomach.

"Look, you can tell me anything. Really. I'm a great listener," Eric urged.

"I know you are. You're amazing. It's just that... well, I don't think I can tell you this." In spite of her best efforts, her voice shook.

"Have I done something wrong? You can tell me that, too, you know. I would never intentionally do anything to upset you." His forehead wrinkled with worry. "So, if it's me, just let me know."

"No, Eric, you haven't done anything wrong. In fact, the problem is that you've done everything right. For months now, ever since I've arrived, you've just been... perfect."

Her eyes filled with tears. She tried her hardest to

blink them away, but several spilled out and ran down her cheeks.

"Gemma, please don't cry. I can't handle seeing you upset." He reached over and wiped away her tears with his thumbs.

"I'm not upset. I mean, clearly I'm a little upset at the moment. But it's just that I'm mostly...."

"Mostly what?"

"Confused. I'm so confused, Eric. And guilty. The guilt just eats me up inside," she blurted.

"Confused and guilty about what?"

Taking a deep breath, she looked him directly in the eye.

"About you, Eric. For someone who is so perceptive, you seem to have missed the elephant in the room."

The words settled into the quietness of the space. Neither spoke. They simply watched each other, wondering what came next.

"Oh... I see." Eric rose from the bench and began to pace. "Me. You're feeling confused and guilty about me. This is my fault."

"Eric, I don't think this is anyone's fault. It just... is." She shrugged.

"I never meant to make you feel confused. And I certainly never wanted to make you feel guilty." He plopped back down on the bench and faced her again.

"Look, I like you, Eric."

"You do?" His face lit up like a thousand-watt light bulb.

"I do. I like you a whole lot, as a matter of fact. And I don't think I'm wrong in saying that I think you like me too."

"You're not wrong. Not at all. I have very definite... feelings for you."

"I know. But I just have to get this out in the open."

"You can tell me."

"Okay, here's the truth. I'm not ready for a relationship yet. And I don't know when I will be. I'm sorry." Gemma put it all on the table before she could change her mind.

"Gemma, you don't have to apologize to me. Ever. Especially for your feelings."

"Really?"

"Look, I get it. You're still grieving the death of your husband. Sure, it's been over a year, but you loved him a lot longer than that. I will never get in the way or rush you into anything. I'm here for you. I'll be your friend, and only your friend, until you tell me you want something different," he assured her.

"For real? I mean, I like you, Eric. A lot. I feel like I might even be on my way to more than liking you. But... I'm sort of a mess. I would never ask you to wait for... something... with me," Gemma replied.

"You didn't ask. I offered. And the offer stands. I'm not going anywhere."

Eric reached over and sandwiched her small hands inside his large, work-worn, calloused ones.

"You're really something, you know that?" She swallowed hard, trying to keep the tears at bay. "You're sure you want to wait around for me to figure myself out?"

"I've been waiting for you my whole life, Gemma. A little bit longer isn't going to hurt me." He grinned.

~

Eric glanced past Gemma, and he smiled. What she couldn't have known was that her grandmother was inside the greenhouse, surveying their work.

"You watch her, Eric," Emerald said quietly. "They're coming for her, and she's going to need you."

Sixteen

The following week, late one night, long after she and Opal had eaten dinner, Gemma was in her room staring at her computer screen once again, trying to write. Opal was in her own room, working on homework and talking on the phone with Ryder. Gemma heard her daughter laugh periodically, marveling at how much the girl had changed since their arrival in Beacon Shores.

Maybe it was the house, or living next to the ocean, or the small-town environment. Maybe it was simply the fact that she had Ryder. All Gemma knew was that she was grateful Opal was happy. There had been a time, not so long ago, when she believed she'd never see her daughter smile again.

Things were finally falling into place for them, it

seemed. Now if Gemma could make some headway on her novel, life would really be looking up. She had finally settled on the fact that she was going to write a fictionalized version of Pearl's life. She felt inspired and led in that direction, and she was going to follow. It was where her mind was these days, so she decided to focus her efforts there.

Pearl's journal had been such an inspiration to her, and Gemma believed she was meant to find it. She was so swept up in Pearl's story and shocked at the various ways her great-great-grandmother's life paralleled her own. It was almost eerie at times how much the women had in common. Flipping to the next page in the journal, Gemma began to read.

Ru and Amie are quick learners. It's obvious that healing is in their blood. Of course, being the children of two Braucherei parents isn't common. Maybe it makes them stronger. I worry that it will make them targets. They know almost as many charms as I do, and their affinity for plants and herbal tinctures is really quite remarkable. Amie is a young woman now, and before long, I will hand the reins over to her. She has a young man whom she adores, and they've been spending much time together. I pray our family traditions will continue with her and her children. And my dear little Ru! She's such a strong-spirited girl. I have no idea where the years will take her, but I imagine she'll be leaving her mark on this world for some time to come.

Gemma stopped reading and let the information sink in. Pearl had taught her daughters her healing methods. Eric said the gifts had been passed down through the women in Gemma's family, so it would make sense that Pearl would have taught Ru and Amie.

Since she had first read the word *Braucherei*, Gemma had been researching the practice. She discovered that Braucherei, a system of traditional folk magic in the Pennsylvania Dutch culture, was still used in the present day in some areas. It seemed extraordinary that a practice originating in Pennsylvania had made its way to the Washington coast all those years ago.

For the sake of her own curiosity, as well as book research, Gemma had been educating herself on the topic. The things she had learned were eye-opening. It was really no wonder the people of Beacon Shores had always believed her family was strange. Back in Pearl's time, having beliefs and traditions so far off the beaten path had probably been outright dangerous. It made her admire Pearl even more for holding fast to her ways and passing them on to her daughters.

Gemma flipped forward in the journal and continued reading.

Sterling has stayed, but for how long? My heart

breaks with the knowledge that he'll eventually have to leave Moonstone House, but I try not to think of that. Instead, I focus on being happy with him for whatever time we have together. It's taken me a while to release the guilt, but loving Sterling has brought me back to life. After Robert's death, I didn't believe that was possible.

I said before that I knew Sterling had some sort of intense magic, and I was right. He finally confided his secret to me—he can speak to those who have gone on before us. Sterling is a medium. He has the ability to talk to the dead. It's something I don't understand, but nevertheless, I believe he's telling me the truth. Spiritualism has begun to spread in America, and Sterling is paid generously by the wealthy for his ability to communicate with the dead. He says there are many imposters, but his power is true.

He gave me a large box containing a gift, one I will never be able to repay. He said I must hide it safely away for a rainy day.

Gemma stopped reading as her thoughts whirled in her mind. *Was Sterling some sort of con artist? What was the gift he gave Pearl that she needed to hide?* As always, she had more questions than answers after reading Pearl's journal.

Snapping the book shut, she placed it in the dresser drawer. She was about to climb into bed when she heard a sound that caused the hairs on her arms to stand on end. It was the young girl's voice singing the unsettling song, the one she'd heard right after moving in.

"Listen close and you'll find me,
Buried 'neath the Remembering Tree.
Tucked inside and nestled deep,
Buried 'neath the Remembering Tree.
Hearts of hatred, hearts of greed
Seek the treasure buried deep.
Only she who holds the key
Will unearth the secrets of the Remembering Tree."

Sweat beads gathered on Gemma's upper lip, and her heart pounded in her chest.

Where is the voice coming from? Is someone inside the house?

Gathering her courage, she walked quickly down the hall toward Opal's room. She listened closely but only heard silence. No one was moving around. Her daughter's room was quiet. Opening the bedroom door slowly, Gemma saw that Opal was asleep. Her steady, even breathing indicated she'd been out for a while. Clearly her daughter hadn't heard the girl's singing.

Closing the door without a sound, Gemma crept down the hall, turning on the lights in all the other bedrooms. No one was there, but the singing had started once again. She glanced over the banister, looking into the darkness below. *Why didn't I put a night-light down there?*

Knowing she had to find the source of the singing, Gemma took a deep breath and descended the staircase. When she reached the bottom, she quickly flipped on the overhead light, illuminating the living room. It was empty. Continuing her search, she investigated the sitting room, the kitchen, the mudroom, the laundry room, and the downstairs bathroom. She even opened the jelly closet. They were all empty.

With trembling hands, she opened the front door and stepped outside. The singing grew louder. Following the sound, Gemma crossed the front porch and walked down the stairs. Her bare feet grew damp from the dew that had settled upon the grass.

Movement in her peripheral vision caused her to turn her head toward the redbud tree. The song was deafeningly loud as Gemma inched forward, moving slowly toward the tree. She stifled a scream when she saw a swinging scarecrow, hanging by the neck, on the lowest branch of the redbud tree.

The singing stopped as suddenly as it had begun.

Her body trembling, Gemma grabbed the bottom of the scarecrow and pulled it down. Shining the flashlight from her phone toward the object, she gasped as the form grew clear. Crouching to get a better look, she saw the effigy had been draped with an old-fashioned scrap of material resembling a dress. The hanging rope was looped around its neck, and a sign was tacked to the front of its dress.

It said "HANG THE WITCH."

Seventeen

Gemma sat at the kitchen table, nursing her third cup of coffee, praying for the first light of morning to come quickly. She had been awake all night long, unable to get the strange singing and the witch in the tree out of her mind. She had gone upstairs to try to sleep but had simply lain there in the dark, eyes wide with fear, startling at every strange noise she heard.

Finally, at around five o'clock, she'd crept downstairs and made a pot of coffee. She thought about the effigy in the tree and shuddered. She'd hidden it in a box on the porch, not quite sure what to do with it. Who would do such a thing? She barely even knew anyone in Beacon Shores.

Her first thought when she'd seen it was to call

Eric, but it was already well past 11:00 p.m., so she'd thought better of it, not wanting to wake him. She knew he would have been there in minutes, though, if she'd made the call. She had no doubt.

Eric always showed up around seven in the morning, so she decided to wait and tell him about it then. To keep her mind off things, she'd typed away at her laptop for the past two hours, working on her book, hoping that focusing on Pearl's life would help her forget about her own.

When six thirty rolled around, she heard Opal rummaging around in her room upstairs, getting ready for school. Opal and Ryder always arrived a bit early and played music outside before school started. Gemma was glad her daughter was oblivious to what had happened. Opal had no idea about the night she'd had, and Gemma planned to keep it that way.

Thirty minutes later, Opal came downstairs, grabbed the breakfast Gemma had prepared for her, kissed her mother goodbye, and headed out the door to school. Not even five minutes later, she heard the crunch of gravel as Eric's truck pulled into the driveway. She waited, his steaming coffee mug in her hands, for him to knock twice on the door and call, "Hello," as he came into the kitchen. Their morning routine was well rehearsed.

As he walked into the kitchen, his warm smile immediately disappeared when he saw Gemma. She had tried her best to conceal her emotions, and though she had been mildly successful with Opal, Eric picked up on her state of mind immediately.

"What's wrong?" he asked, forehead creased with concern as he gently took his coffee mug from her hands. "You look like you've been awake all night."

"I have been," she answered, sinking into the dining room chair.

"What happened?" He sipped his coffee and settled his kind eyes on her.

"Something really strange and scary," Gemma began.

"Tell me."

"Well, I was upstairs writing late last night, and I heard something really weird. It was a girl singing."

"A girl singing?"

"Yes." She nodded. "It was this odd song. I actually heard it once before, right after I first moved in, but I never figured out where it was coming from then either."

"Why didn't you tell me about it when it happened the first time?" Eric asked, tilting his head to the side.

"I barely knew you then. I didn't want you to

think I was completely off my rocker. Even if I am." She rolled her eyes. "Anyway, I went through the whole house looking for where the singing was coming from. No one was there, and Opal was sound asleep. I searched inside the house, and then I went outside."

"And?"

"There was a scarecrow-like thing hanging, with a noose around its neck, from the branch of the redbud tree. It was wearing some sort of makeshift dress, and it had a sign attached with the words *HANG THE WITCH* written on it." Gemma finished quickly, blurting everything out before she could think twice.

"Someone hung an effigy of a witch in the redbud tree?" The muscles in Eric's jaw tensed as he clenched his teeth.

"Mmm-hmm." She nodded, her eyes filling with tears.

"And you didn't see anyone? You don't know who it was?"

"No. But I was honestly so scared by that point that I didn't go out looking," she answered, her voice quivering. "I came inside and locked the doors."

"Thank goodness for that." He dragged his hands through his hair in frustration.

"I put the thing in a box on the porch if you want

to see it. I'd prefer not to look at it again," she added quietly.

"Gemma, why didn't you call me last night when this happened?" Eric leaned toward her and clasped her trembling hands tightly in his own.

"It was late. I didn't want to wake you," she offered softly. "I didn't want to be a bother."

"Ah, honey, you could never be a bother, not even if you tried."

He stood from his chair and leaned down, wrapping his arms around her from behind as she sat at the table. She relaxed into his embrace, feeling safe and sound for the first time in hours. After a couple minutes, he sat back down at the table.

Gemma continued, "I don't understand why someone would do that. Just to scare me? A prank by a bunch of kids or something? And the singing... that freaks me out almost as much as the hanging witch. I mean, it was so... *real.*"

"I wish I knew. I don't have an answer, but I plan to get to the bottom of it, so don't you worry about it for another second," Eric encouraged, the muscles in his jaw tightening.

"I'll try, but I doubt I'm going to be able to pull that off." She smiled weakly.

The sound of a car coming down the driveway

caused them both to stand quickly. They walked out onto the porch together. Gemma frowned and Eric swore under his breath when they saw the Tesla.

"What does he want?" she asked.

"Nothing good," he gritted between clenched teeth.

"Good morning," Dominic called as he walked toward them.

"I thought I told you to get lost," Eric returned.

"And I thought this wasn't your house. I'm here to talk to Gemma," Dominic replied easily.

"I don't think we have anything to talk about," she answered. "Why are you here at seven thirty in the morning?"

"I wanted to check back with you and see if you've had time to consider my offer." Dominic grinned, leaning casually on the porch railing. "And I'm an early riser. You know what they say? 'The early bird gets the worm' and all that."

"I told you before, I'm not selling," Gemma replied.

"And I told you that I would check back again, so that's what I'm doing."

"My answer hasn't changed," she said stubbornly.

"Well, I'm having a hard time understanding why this is such a difficult choice for you. It's a lot of money. Far more than what it's worth," Dominic explained, his smile faltering a bit.

"I'm not selling," she repeated.

"I'll double the offer, then," he said more forcefully, his face turning red.

"Not interested," Gemma shot back.

"Stubborn woman!" Dominic spat the words at her. "I should have known you'd be just like the rest of them."

"The rest of who?" Gemma asked.

"Bad seeds! All of you!" he yelled, his face contorting with rage. "The women in your family are nothing but trouble. You'll get what's coming to you. I promise you that."

Anger bubbled inside Gemma, her fear momentarily forgotten. She stepped toward Dominic, but when she got close, everything became blurry and time seemed to warp. She was staring at him one second, then someone else the next. The man in front of her looked similar to Dominic, but he was dressed strangely, like someone from the past. The man was holding an old-fashioned lantern and screaming, "Thou shalt not suffer a witch to live," as an angry crowd pressed in behind him.

Gasping in shock, Gemma stepped away from

Dominic, tripping in her haste. Eric's strong arms caught her from behind, holding her upright.

Eric steadied her, but once he knew Gemma was fine, he placed himself between her and Dominic. Fury rolled off Eric's body in waves as he stalked toward the other man without hesitation.

Dominic, clearly sensing that Eric had reached his limit, took a couple steps backward.

"How dare you come to Gemma's house and threaten her? I guess that's what the men in your family do, though, right? Threaten innocent women? Get out of here and leave her alone. Next time we see you anywhere on the property, we're calling the police."

Eric never raised his voice, but his anger was palpable, seething, and growing in intensity.

Dominic must have decided he'd officially worn out his welcome, because he stalked to his car, climbed inside, slammed the door, and pulled out of the driveway without another word.

Once he was gone, Gemma walked over and stood beside Eric. She was about to speak, but when she looked at his face, she could see he was somewhere else, light-years away.

"Dogan Becker," Eric said quietly, his eyes focused on something far in the distance. "Yes, I know. I will."

"Eric? Are you okay?" She gently placed her hand on his arm.

Blinking a few times, he focused his gaze on Gemma. Suddenly, he was back with her. "Yeah, I'm fine. I can't believe that jerk had the nerve to come back here. Are you okay?"

"I'm actually more worried about you at the moment," she said. "What happened just now? It seemed like you were somewhere else. Talking to someone else. And you said someone's name."

"It's nothing." Eric smiled, clearly trying to brush her comment aside.

"It's something," Gemma insisted.

"Ah, Gemma, I don't want to get into it right now," he answered.

"Tell me, please? I'm worried about you. You look like you saw a ghost," she continued.

Sighing heavily, Eric replied, "That's because I did."

Eighteen

"You saw a ghost?" Gemma pressed, leading Eric back inside the house and closing the door behind them. "Can you tell me what you mean by that?"

She walked toward the living room, and he followed. Sitting down on the sofa, she patted the cushion, motioning for him to sit beside her. Plopping onto the couch, Eric let out a long sigh. His eyes met hers, and there was a look of uncertainty and hesitation she'd never seen before.

"Gemma, can't we please just let this go?"

"We can if that's what you really want. But I would like it even more if you felt comfortable enough to tell me what you meant," she answered gently.

"I don't know if you're ready to hear it. And I don't know if I'm ready to say it," Eric hedged.

"You can tell me anything, Eric."

"I just... I don't want what I say to... change anything between us. I don't want you to look at me any... differently than how you always have," he stammered.

"I don't have a clue what you're going to say, Eric, but I honestly can't think of anything you could tell me that would change the way I see you. You're a kind, generous, caring man. What could possibly change that?"

Gemma took a deep breath, reached over, and threaded her fingers through Eric's. They rested their intertwined hands on his leg. Her heart beat wildly inside her chest. She had the feeling they were about to completely blur the lines of their friendship, and she wasn't sure how she felt about that. But it didn't stop her from scooting closer to him.

"I'm not sure you understand what you're asking for, but I guess maybe it's time to tell you." Eric paused, taking a deep breath before continuing, "Gemma, I'm about to go all *Sixth Sense* on you...."

"What's that mean?" She chuckled.

"It means that I, uh, I see dead people."

"You see dead people? I'm not sure I follow." Gemma shook her head slowly.

"Ghosts... people who have passed on... you know, dead people. I see them. I can talk to them. And what's even crazier, they talk to me."

Gemma looked closely at Eric, trying to determine if he was messing with her. His face remained impassive, not a trace of a smile to be found.

"You... you're, um... you're serious?"

"I am. This is something I take very seriously. It's also something not everyone understands or believes in, so I get it if you think it's all a bit too 'out there' for you," he explained.

Her thoughts were racing, running a mile a minute inside her brain. She had a million questions, a thousand reasons why what he was saying shouldn't make sense to her. Did she even believe that people could talk to the dead? She'd honestly never given it much thought before, but looking at Eric, sitting next to her, squeezing her hand, his heart on his sleeve, she realized that she believed him completely.

"Can you say something? Please?" He spoke quietly, a slight tremor in his voice. "Say anything. Tell me I'm crazy or whatever. Just say something."

"I don't think you're crazy, Eric," Gemma said slowly.

"I have questions, for sure, but I don't think you're lying, or that you're out of your mind or anything like that. I don't think about you any differently than I did before."

"You have no idea what that means to me."

He squeezed her hand tightly, and she scooted even closer to him.

"Can you tell me a little bit about your... special gift?" she asked.

"Well, all the men in my family are mediums. Pretty much as far back as I know. It's just something we've always been able to do." He shrugged. "My dad helped me learn about my gift when I was a kid."

"That's fascinating. Truly. I knew you were special, Eric, but this is sort of beyond anything I would have thought of."

"It's just part of who I am."

"Can you tell me how it happens? Like... I don't know, do people come to you and ask you to find a person who's died and talk to them? Or do the ghosts just appear to you somehow?"

"It's not anything I've ever really advertised, so most people have no idea about it. Outside of my immediate family, you're the only person I've ever told," he confessed.

"Wow. Really?"

"Really. It's kind of a private, sensitive subject, so it's not something I'm comfortable sharing."

"I'm so sorry. I didn't mean to make you feel like you had to tell me."

"I wouldn't have told you if I didn't want to, Gemma. I've always known I would tell you about it eventually, I just wasn't sure when."

She squeezed his hand. "Thank you for trusting me."

"I trust you completely."

Gemma's stomach flipped somersaults as Eric's all-knowing eyes drank her in. Ever so slowly, as if they were being pulled together by a magnetic force, their faces inched closer. Before she was able to stop herself, or second-guess what she was doing, she closed the gap between them. She let go of his hand, wrapped her arm around his neck, and pulled Eric's face to hers, her lips grazing his gently. The kiss was soft and filled with promise. When it ended, she was speechless, stunned by her own boldness.

"I've wanted to do that for a very long time," Eric said quietly, a smile working at the corners of his mouth.

"Me too," Gemma replied, smoothing her hair and trying to force a smile of her own as the guilt began to settle in.

"Uh-oh. What's wrong? The look on your face just went from happy to worried all in the course of a second. Something is bugging you."

"It's just that... I've pretty much wanted to kiss you since the first day I saw you too. And the idea of that makes me feel just a little bit... I don't know... guilty." She shrugged, struggling to meet Eric's eyes.

"Can you tell me why you feel guilty?" he asked gently.

"In one word—Clayton. I haven't kissed another man since I was twenty. And I know Clay is dead, but I can't help but feel that I'm betraying him somehow," she confessed.

"I understand."

"I guess I'm afraid to move on. It feels wrong, like I'm leaving him behind."

"Do you think Clayton feels like you're leaving him behind?"

"How am I supposed to know that? I mean, I have no idea how he'd feel. This isn't something we ever talked about. I never planned for him to die."

Eric shifted in his seat and glanced past Gemma. A strange look washed over his face.

"You know Clayton would want you to be happy, right?" he said slowly, still looking past her.

"Maybe. I guess? I mean, I don't know." She shrugged.

"I do."

"How could you possibly know?"

"Because he's here. Right now. He's in the room with us," Eric answered, finally locking eyes with Gemma.

"Clayton is here?" Her voice trembled, and she swiveled her body, looking around the room.

"He is. I can see him."

"You can see Clay?" Gemma's hand fluttered to her mouth. She nervously chewed on her fingernails. "Can I… can I talk to him?"

"Of course. What do you want to say to him?"

"I want him to know… well… that I miss him. So much. I think I'll never stop missing him," she began, her tears creeping in, making speech difficult.

"He says he misses you too. You and Opal," Eric said. "He also says he's sorry he had to leave you."

"Oh, Clay," Gemma cried.

"He wants you to know he loves you, and he knows you love him too."

"I do. I'll always love him—" Her voice broke.

"Most of all, he'd like me to tell you that he hopes you're happy, that you'll move on with your life, with his blessing," he continued.

Gemma covered her face with her hands and sobbed. Eric rubbed her back in even, soothing strokes.

"He has to go now, Gemma, but he says you'll always be his favorite girl," he added.

"He used to say that to me all the time. How could you have known that?" She wiped her face with her palms, smiling through her tears. "Is he still there?"

"No. He's gone."

"I-I don't even know what to say. I don't know how to thank you for that. It's like a gift I never thought I'd get."

"I'm glad I could give that to you."

"Have you seen him... Clay...before? I'm not sure how this works."

"Not until today. I think he showed up because you were upset and I was receptive to listening for him. I can't stand to see you sad, and I was hoping that maybe I could reach out to him, and that he could tell you for himself that you have nothing to feel guilty about. I'm glad it worked."

"Me too. That helps a lot, actually. I mean, my feelings for you don't seem to be going away, and my guilt seemed pretty stuck too. It sounds like maybe I can let go of that now," Gemma said quietly, hyperaware of what that meant for them.

"I'll never push you. Never. We can take things

slowly and see where we end up. You're free to take the lead, and I'm more than happy to follow."

Smiling slowly, Gemma moved closer to Eric. "Then follow my lead on this," she whispered as she placed her lips on his.

Nineteen

Gemma and Eric were sharing a cup of coffee and chatting about the things they'd discovered about each other when a forgotten thought popped back into her head.

"So, we got a little sidetracked, which I'm not complaining about, but you never told me about what happened with you when we were on the porch. You know, when Dominic was here."

"Dominic," he said through gritted teeth. "That man makes me want to shove my fist through the wall."

"Me too, but maybe we could not do that. I mean, think of all the hours we've spent fixing this place up. The last thing we need is to have to patch a hole in the wall." Gemma laughed.

"You're right, I guess. I'd still like the satisfaction of knocking out a few of those perfect teeth of his."

"I can't say I'd be opposed to watching you do that. But I digress." She giggled. "When we were out on the porch, I remember you said a man's name. Can you tell me what that was about?"

"Dogan Becker," Eric replied. "That's the name I said."

"Yeah, that's it. Who's that?"

"Dogan Becker would have been Dominic's great-great-grandfather. He was the mayor of Beacon Shores when Pearl was alive."

"Really? How do you know that?"

"Well... Emerald told me."

"Emerald, as in my grandmother?" Gemma raised her eyebrows in surprise.

"One and the same."

"So, you've seen my grandmother too?"

"All the time. Emerald and I were great friends when she was alive. I think that's why my connection to her is so strong, even now that she's gone. We have pretty regular conversations, as strange as I know that must sound to you," he explained.

"I had no idea. I mean, sure, it's kind of weird, but I think it's super cool that you can see and talk to my grandmother. I wish I could. So, what did she say about Dogan Becker, then?"

"She said he's the man who turned Beacon Shores against Pearl. He's the one who started the whole mess about the town hating the women in your family. As the mayor, he had some pull, and people listened to him."

Gemma thought back to what happened when she'd stepped close to Dominic. She'd seen a man in outdated clothing screaming, "Thou shalt not suffer a witch to live," while an angry mob pressed in behind him. Had she somehow caught a glimpse of Dogan Becker?

"Well, if Dogan was anything like his great-great-grandson, I'm pretty sure I wouldn't have liked him one bit," she replied.

"I can almost guarantee you wouldn't have liked him. And he would have hated you."

"What makes you say that?"

"Because men like Dogan and Dominic Becker can't stand strong women. They scare them to death," Eric answered.

"But not you, right?" Gemma grinned. "You're not scared of me, are you?"

"I'm terrified of you. But not because you're strong. I like that."

"Then why?"

"Because you have the ability to consume me completely. I'm pretty sure you have already."

"Good answer." She smiled as a warm, contented feeling washed over her.

They talked some more about the Beckers' vendetta against the women in her family, and then Eric decided it was time for him to get to work.

Gemma's phone buzzed, and she saw there was a text from Abigail, Ryder's mom.

Abigail: Looking forward to dinner at Moonstone House tonight. Can't wait to see what you've done with the place. I'll bring dessert.

Gemma: Great! See you at six.

Gemma shook her head. She'd completely forgotten she'd invited them over! It was a good thing Abigail had sent the text; otherwise, they would have shown up to no dinner. She sighed heavily.

"Everything okay?" Eric asked, standing to rinse his coffee mug.

"Yeah, it's fine. It's just that I invited Abigail and Ryder to dinner tonight, and I totally forgot about it until I got her text saying she would bring dessert." Gemma rolled her eyes.

"That sounds nice. I'm sure you'll have a great time, even if you forgot about it." He smiled.

"I also forgot to invite you, which I fully intended to do. Can you come?" she asked, her voice hopeful.

"Sure. What time? And what should I bring?"

"Six o'clock, and just bring yourself. I'll take care of the rest."

"You sure?"

"Of course I'm sure. You're going to be here working all day. You don't need to worry about bringing food. I'll run into town and grab supplies and whip up something fabulous." Gemma grinned, excited to share her home with her new friends.

"Great. I'll run home to shower after work, and I'll be back around six. Will that be okay?"

"That will be perfect."

"I'm going to get to work, then." He smiled and turned to leave.

"Eric." Gemma cleared her throat. "Aren't you forgetting something?"

"What?"

"This."

She walked toward him and wrapped her arms around his neck. Standing on her tiptoes, she kissed him gently.

Twenty

Gemma rushed around the kitchen at a quarter to six, putting the finishing touches on dinner. She'd decided to make seafood pasta, salad, and some homemade biscuits, and everything smelled delicious. Opal set the table while Gemma grated a pile of parmesan cheese.

"Thanks for your help, honey." Gemma smiled as Opal arranged the flatware at each place setting.

"It's kind of exciting to have dinner guests coming, isn't it?" Opal grinned.

"It is. We used to do this kind of thing all the time, didn't we? I'd kind of forgotten how much I liked it."

"Me too. I'm glad you and Ryder's mom get along too. That makes things easier," Opal added.

"Things? What sort of things?" Gemma asked with a playful smile.

"Mom, you know what I mean. I like Ryder. A lot. It helps that our parents get along."

"I knew what you meant, honey. I was just teasing you. I'm glad to see you so happy here."

"I really am. I can't believe I'm saying it, but I really love this town." Opal beamed.

Gemma was sprinkling the cheese onto the pasta when she heard Eric's familiar double knock, followed by a "Hello" as he came into the kitchen.

"Hey there." She smiled.

"Hi," Eric said, glancing in Opal's direction.

Gemma waited for him to move closer to her, but he just stood on the other side of the counter, awkwardly holding a bottle of wine. She immediately understood what was going on. Eric wasn't sure if she had told Opal about the fact that the two of them had taken a giant leap over the friendship line.

"Hi, Eric," Opal said as she filled water glasses. "Feel free to kiss my mom if you want to. Just pretend I'm not here."

"I, uh, well...," he stammered.

"It's okay. I told her," Gemma whispered, a mischievous grin tipping up the corners of her mouth.

Eric looked mildly uncomfortable, and Gemma

was about to say something else when the doorbell rang.

"Saved by the bell." Opal giggled as she walked past them to answer the door.

Hugs and pleasantries were exchanged as Opal led Abigail and Ryder into the kitchen. Within seconds, the teenagers disappeared into the sitting room and started messing around on the piano. Gemma and Eric gave Abigail the grand tour, and then it was time to sit down to dinner. Plates of seafood pasta were consumed in record time, and the dinner conversation never lagged. Gemma couldn't believe how good and comfortable it felt to have guests at her table. It was clearly something she'd been missing.

"Mom, can we be excused?" Opal asked.

"We want to work on the song some more," Ryder added.

"Of course you can." Gemma smiled as the teenagers quickly ducked out of the room and headed for the piano.

"That was delicious, Gemma. Really," Abigail said as she placed her napkin on her plate. "You're a great cook."

"Yeah, it was really good," Ryder chimed in.

"Thanks. Cooking lets me zone out and get

outside of my head for a bit. It's relaxing for me," Gemma replied.

"Feel free to cook for me anytime, then." Eric laughed. "I mean, I want you to feel relaxed. If eating delicious food is the price I have to pay to make that happen for you, then so be it."

"A real hero, this one." Abigail giggled. "Really taking one for the team."

"I help out however I—" Eric began.

His sentence was cut short by a crashing sound and breaking glass in the living room. Eric shot like a rocket out of his chair and ran into the room. The remnants of shattered panes of glass from the large bay window were scattered across the floor.

"Oh no!" Gemma cried. "What happened?"

"Stay back," Eric instructed as he walked toward the window. Crouching down, he grabbed a large object off the floor. "This happened."

"What is it?" Opal asked as she and Ryder came into the living room. She grabbed Gemma's hand and squeezed it tightly. "We heard it from the other room."

Gemma could feel the tension and anger rippling off Eric's body as he walked toward her, the object resting in the palms of both of his hands. Leaning toward him to get a look, she saw it was a sizable rock with the word WITCH painted in large block letters.

"Who would do this?" Gemma asked, her eyes filling with tears as she looked at the shattered glass on her floor.

"I'll give you one guess," Eric answered through gritted teeth. "And I'm calling the police."

"Did you see someone? Was there a car?" Abigail asked.

"No car. We would have heard it. He came here on foot," Eric replied.

"He? Who are you talking about, Eric?" Abigail asked.

"Becker."

"Dominic?"

"Yes," Eric answered.

"What makes you think it was him?" Abigail questioned.

"I don't think it was him. I know it was," Eric seethed.

"C'mon, Eric. I mean, sure, the guy's a jerk. Always has been. But do you really think he'd do this?" Abigail asked, gesturing toward the window.

"Yes. I have no doubt."

"What makes you so sure? Am I missing something here?" Abigail raised an eyebrow, looking between Eric and Gemma.

"He's been here a couple times, wanting to buy

Moonstone House," Gemma explained. "He's been quite persistent. He was really angry when I refused."

"Angry enough to throw a rock through our window? And why does it say 'WITCH'?" Opal asked, her eyes wide with fear.

"The men in the Becker family have a problem with the women in yours," Eric said. "It goes back generations. I'm calling the police now."

Without another word, he stalked toward the kitchen, muttering to himself. A few moments later, Gemma heard him talking to someone, presumably the police, explaining what happened and giving them the address.

"I'm sorry about this, you guys. It was such a great night up until this." Gemma motioned toward the broken window.

"Ah, sweetie, don't apologize. We had a wonderful time. We're just sorry this happened to you," Abigail said, hugging her tightly.

Gemma glanced at Opal, who was being similarly comforted by Ryder.

"The police are on their way," Eric said as he came back into the living room. "I asked them if you needed to stay, Abbie, and they said you could go on home. It may be a while before they get here."

"Do you want me to stay? I can if you'd like, Gemma," Abigail asked.

"Thank you, but that's not necessary. There's no need for you to sit around waiting for the police. You can't tell them anything more than we can. Go on home," Gemma replied.

"I don't like this at all. It doesn't feel safe for you to stay here, Gemma," Abigail countered.

"We'll be fine," Gemma returned, wishing she felt a bit more confident in what she was saying.

"Then at least let me take Opal to our house. I have a guest room she can stay in. That way you can handle things here and not have to worry about her safety for tonight," Abigail offered.

"That's a great idea, actually. Thank you." Gemma sighed. "Is that okay with you, Opal?"

"I guess so. But maybe I should stay here with you, Mom. I don't want you to be alone with all this," Opal answered.

"She won't be alone, sweetheart. I'm not going anywhere. After the police come, I'm going to board up that window and sleep on the couch," Eric explained.

Feeling like a deflated balloon, Gemma didn't even have the strength to argue with him. She was just glad she didn't have to face the rest of the night alone.

Opal packed a bag, kissed her mother, and then she, Ryder, and Abigail headed out after another round of hugs. Not sure what to do with herself, Gemma went to clean up the remnants of dinner. Eric rolled up his sleeves and did the same as they waited for the police to come.

The two worked side by side, neither saying a word. A thousand thoughts raced through Gemma's head, but she couldn't bring herself to give voice to any of them. It seemed best to say nothing at all.

About thirty minutes later, the police arrived. Two officers scoured every inch of the house, inside and outside, and questioned both Gemma and Eric extensively.

Eric told them about his suspicions of Dominic Becker, and the officers assured him they would follow up with questioning him. Gemma didn't hold out much hope. After all, Dominic was a very powerful man. He had money and connections aplenty. Short of him admitting to it, which he wasn't going to do, there was little to no chance that Dominic Becker was going to be held responsible for doing this. They had no proof other than their own suspicions.

The officers gave Gemma their contact information and left. Eric went outside to the shed and carried in several large pieces of plywood. Together, they boarded up the broken bay window. Gemma fought back tears the whole time.

"You don't have to stay here, you know. I'll be fine," she said, trying to put on a brave face. She didn't want to burden Eric with her problems.

"Of course I'm staying here. I'm not about to leave you alone. This is the second thing that's happened in as many days. Clearly someone is after you. And we both know who it is."

"Don't sleep on the couch, then. I have a guest room, you know. At least sleep in there."

"I'm staying down here. I want to be ready in case he comes back."

Sighing heavily, Gemma conceded. "I'll go grab some blankets and pillows."

She went upstairs and dug through the linen closet. Arms full, she trudged back downstairs and began making Eric a bed on the couch. Not sure what else to do, Gemma decided she would turn in for the night, although she knew sleep wasn't going to come easily.

"You should go to bed. You look exhausted," Eric said, pulling her close to him and holding her tightly. "I'm going to be right here, so you can rest easy."

"I don't think that's a possibility, but I'll try," she answered.

He leaned down and kissed her softly. "I'm not going to let anything happen to you. I promise."

Gemma headed upstairs to her room, took a quick shower, and tried to wash the day away. Then she threw on her most comfortable flannel pajamas and climbed beneath her covers. Placing her phone on the bedside table, she turned off the lamp and lay in the darkness, her head swimming with questions. Deep down, she knew Dominic was behind both the witch in the redbud tree and the rock through the window. He was trying to scare her into doing what he wanted.

"Well, Dominic Becker, that's not going to happen. Moonstone House belongs to me, and I'm not going anywhere," she whispered into the darkness. "You want a fight? You've got one."

Twenty-One

It was a good ninety minutes before Gemma finally managed to slip into a deep sleep, but as soon as she did, her subconscious immediately took over. With a start, she opened her eyes. She was in her bedroom at Moonstone House, but everything was different. The bed frame was the same, but her down comforter was missing. In its place was a patchwork quilt. Confused, she ran her hand across the wall, searching for the light switch, but she found none. Instead, a kerosene lamp flickered on the small bedside table next to her. She picked up the lamp, trying to steady her shaking hands.

Telling herself not to panic, Gemma tiptoed down the hallway toward Opal's room. Opening the door, she peeked inside and saw a teenage girl sleeping there, but it wasn't her daughter. Heart racing, she opened the door to the bedroom beside it, the guest room. Holding up the lamp, she peered inside. There was another girl sleeping in that bed, a younger one, someone else she didn't know.

Disoriented, Gemma crept down the stairs, the shadows on the wall dancing eerily as the kerosene lamp dimly lit her path. Reaching the living room, she noticed her sofa wasn't there, and Eric wasn't asleep on it. In its place she saw a large armchair and an old rocker. The bay window was intact, not a sliver of shattered glass to be seen. None of her decorations hung on the wall, and Opal's piano wasn't there in the adjoining sitting room.

Taking a shuddering breath, she went into the kitchen. Disbelief washed over her when she saw none of her appliances. There was an old-fashioned wood-burning stove where her electric range should have been, and there wasn't a refrigerator in sight. Turning slowly in a circle, she took note of her missing microwave, toaster, and coffeepot.

"What's happening?" Gemma whispered.

Knowing she should stay inside, but needing to figure out what was going on, she opened the door and walked quietly onto the front porch. Things outside looked mostly the same, yet slightly different. The greenhouse was missing, but in its place was a lush garden, filled with every kind of plant and herb one could imagine.

All at once, Gemma noticed a light in the barn. Creeping quietly in that direction, she plastered herself against the outside of the barn door, close to the wall where she hoped to remain hidden. She heard voices. Peeking through a small crack in the wall, she peered inside.

There was a man and a woman, standing closely together, nearly embracing. Trying to calm her racing heart, she leaned in a little closer, hoping to hear what they were saying.

"A gift? For me? You didn't have to do that," the woman said.

"There is no one else in the world I'd rather give this to," the man answered. "Open it. Look inside."

Gemma heard a slight creak as the woman opened the large wooden box.

"Sterling," the woman gasped. "I can't accept this. It's far too valuable."

"Pearl, take it. Please. There may come a time when you'll need it. As much as I want to, I won't always be around to take care of you. This will help you and the girls," he explained.

"But I'd rather have you," Pearl said quietly.

"I'd rather be with you than anywhere else on Earth, but we both know that isn't going to be possible in the same way for much longer. This is the one way I can help you. Please, let me help you."

Gemma moved in a little closer, placing her face farther into the crack in the wall. All at once, Sterling glanced her way, making direct eye contact with her. His ocean eyes bored into hers, and she gasped, the force of his gaze taking her breath away.

"Eric," she whispered.

He kept his eyes locked on hers and smiled, and the feeling that washed over her was indescribable. But that wasn't Eric. Was it? Pearl had called him Sterling.

Gemma's head began to spin.

Sterling and Pearl?

Where am I?

Better yet, when *am I?*

She opened her eyes quickly as bright sunlight beamed in through her lace curtains. Sitting up in bed with a start, she saw that her bedroom was exactly as it had always been. Looking around, she noticed that everything appeared exactly as it was supposed to. The patchwork quilt was gone, her familiar down comforter in its place. She made note of the light switches on the wall and the absence of any kerosene lamps.

"What a relief." She sighed. "It was all just a dream. A very weird dream."

Gemma swung her legs over the edge of her bed and was about to stand when an object on the bedside table caught her eye. Her hands shook slightly as she reached down and grabbed the old rusted skeleton key lying next to her phone. Shivering as a chill crept down her spine, she turned the key over for inspection. She had no clue where it had come from, but she was very certain of one thing—it hadn't been there when she'd gone to sleep.

Twenty-Two

Gemma dressed quickly, tossed her curls into a messy bun, slipped the skeleton key into the pocket of her jeans, and went downstairs. It was almost seven o'clock, and she knew Eric would be up soon, if he wasn't already.

Sure enough, the sofa was empty, the pile of blankets neatly folded and the pillows stacked on top. Her stomach knotted as she looked at the boarded-up window, a reminder of why Eric was there in the first place. Glancing out the window in the kitchen, she saw him on the ladder, fixing some shingles on one of the outbuildings.

The coffee was already made, thanks to Eric. She poured herself a cup, added a splash of heavy cream, and walked out into the yard.

“’Morning,” he called down to her from the top of the ladder.

“Good morning. Did you get any sleep at all?” Gemma looked up toward Eric, shielding her eyes from the bright sun.

“A little. I was too worked up to sleep much. I kept listening for sounds all night long,” he replied as he managed to sink the nail with just one hit of the hammer.

“I’m sorry you’re caught up in the middle of my mess, Eric. Really.” She shook her head from side to side, anger and frustration churning inside. “This shouldn’t be your problem.”

“Come on, Gemma, stop apologizing.” Eric climbed down the ladder and pulled her into a tight hug. “We’re going to figure this out together. I’d rather be with you than anywhere else on Earth, you know.”

As he spoke, some small, distant memory surfaced. She’d heard that phrase before—last night in her dream. Sterling had said the same words to Pearl.

Reaching into her pocket, Gemma pulled out the skeleton key.

“Does this look familiar at all to you?” She held it up for Eric to see.

He took it from her, placed it in his palm, and inspected it closely. “Hmmm. Should it?”

"I'm not sure," she hedged. "What would a key like that be used for?"

"Could be anything, really. A door, maybe?"

"Possibly."

"The old doors on the inside of the house used to have this kind of lock on them before they were replaced. Could be from that," he offered, dropping the key back into her waiting palm. "Where did you find it?"

"Upstairs," she replied, purposely vague.

"You should hang on to it. They don't make them like that anymore."

"I intend to," she said as she dropped it back into her pocket.

"So, what's your plan for the day?" he inquired.

"I'm going to head into town and go to the historical society. I've been wanting to see what information they have on Moonstone House. Today seems as good a day as any," Gemma answered.

"That's a great plan. It will take your mind off what's going on here. But just so you know, I intend to make myself a permanent fixture on your couch until we figure this mess out. As long as that's all right with you, I mean."

"It's fine with me that you're here. I love having

you around. But I really do wish you'd sleep in the guest room. I hate the thought of you on the sofa."

"We'll see. For now, that's the safest place for me to be until we find out if Becker has any more tricks up his sleeve. Besides, your couch is actually pretty comfortable."

"So is the bed upstairs. But I can see you're set on this, so I won't argue. For now," she replied.

"I just want to be sure nothing happens to you or Opal." Eric shrugged. "I'd never forgive myself if it did."

"I know. And I appreciate it." Gemma stood on her tiptoes and brushed her lips lightly across his. "I'm off to town now."

She went inside, placed the skeleton key in her dresser drawer next to Pearl's journal, grabbed her keys, then walked outside and slid into the car. Starting it up, she headed into town, pulling into the parking lot of the historical society less than ten minutes later.

Twenty-Three

"Can I help you, dear?" the kind-looking older woman asked as Gemma walked through the front door of the Beacon Shores Historical Society.

"I hope so." She smiled. "My name is Gemma Clayborn, and I live at Moonstone House. I'd love to try to find some information about it."

The woman nodded, a smile turning up the corners of her mouth. "Ah, I'm Agnes Daybell. And you must be one of the Jewels."

"The Jewels?" Gemma asked.

"That's what people around here call the women in your family. The Jewels. You know, because you're all named after precious stones and gems and the like?" Agnes laughed.

"Got it. I had no idea people referred to our family that way," Gemma responded. "Very cool."

"Well, if you're looking for information on Moonstone House, you've come to the right place. We have a lot of it. Follow me."

Agnes grabbed her cane and motioned for Gemma to follow her into the back. There was a table and a couple of wooden chairs in the center of the room. Agnes indicated that was where Gemma should work, so she placed her purse and keys on the surface.

"Now, our old newspaper articles will all be on microfiche. I don't suppose you know anything about that, do you?" Agnes asked.

"Actually, I do. I've been a reporter for a very long time, so I know my way around the microfiche," Gemma answered with a laugh.

"A reporter. Nice. Well, I guess I don't need to tell you how to conduct research, then, do I?" Agnes winked.

"Not at all. If you'll just point me in the right direction, I'm pretty good at finding my way through documents and records."

Agnes gave Gemma a quick tour of where everything was kept, and then she returned to her desk.

Gemma decided to start with the old newspaper articles, searching for any information she could find on Dogan Becker. She quickly discovered an abundance of material since the man had been mayor of Beacon Shores. Gemma found one article with a photo of him, and she examined it closely. Goose bumps erupted on her arms as her suspicions were confirmed —Dogan Becker was indeed the man she'd seen during her flashback moment on the porch.

She flipped through several more articles when the headline of a particular one, "Spiritualism in America," caught her attention. Scanning the article quickly, she gasped when she saw the name Sterling E. Johnson. Leaning in closer, she read the article through twice. It was strange, but Gemma came to the conclusion that the man had to be Pearl's Sterling. In her journal, Pearl had written that Sterling said he was a medium, and although Gemma had been skeptical, it seemed Pearl was telling the truth.

It turned out that not only was Sterling a medium, but he was one of the most famous, well-paid ones in the country at that time. Sterling had traveled around the country, state to state, being wined and dined by the wealthiest, most elite members of American society. It seemed the rich upper echelon weren't afraid to pay handsomely for a man like Sterling to connect them to their family members who had passed on to the other side.

Sterling E. Johnson was quite famous, yet also a bit of a mystery. Gemma found more than one article where writers tried to solve the mystery of the man. People speculated that he was anything from a secret European prince to an outright angelic being, and everything in between. She discovered that he had been one of the most celebrated men in America. Gemma wondered about the circumstances that had sent him to Pearl's doorstep, too sick to even walk.

She scrolled through more newspaper articles, finally landing on one that talked about the fire that ravaged the town of Beacon Shores in 1899. She read that the town and nearly everything in it had gone up in flames that fall. Flipping forward a few years, she found another article detailing when it had burned again in 1905. Once again, it was nearly a complete loss.

"That's so odd. What's the likelihood that the same town would burn twice in just a six-year span?" Gemma whispered to herself.

As she dug deeper, she quickly learned she wasn't the only one who found it odd. She ran across an opinion piece written by a woman named Margaret Becker, who just so happened to be the mayor's wife. Gemma reread the final paragraph of the editorial two times, trying to fully absorb its impact.

My fellow citizens, these mysterious circumstances are not so mysterious at all. Our town is at war, and our enemy is not made of flesh and blood. Our enemy is the Evil One and his followers. I beseech you, my friends, we must flush out this wickedness. Do it for yourselves and your children. Do it for the future of Beacon Shores.

"It seems the Beckers have always been obsessed with hunting so-called evil," Gemma said quietly.

She finished reading the article, focusing on the final sentence. Her blood ran cold as she read the last words of Mrs. Becker's opinion piece.

As it says in the Good Book in Exodus 22:18, "Thou shalt not suffer a witch to live."

Twenty-Four

Still unsettled after the disturbing things she'd uncovered at the historical society, Gemma drove toward Moonstone House. She'd learned a lot, but most of the information elicited more questions than answers. It seemed the town—more specifically, the Becker family—had been after the Jewels for generations. But for the life of her, Gemma had no clue why.

Pulling into the driveway, she turned off the car. Tucking the stack of papers she'd copied into her bag, she went inside. She hadn't seen Eric outside, and she wondered where he was. His truck was in the driveway, so he couldn't be far. Depositing her bag and keys onto the kitchen table, she ran upstairs to change. The chilliness of the fall morning had been burned away by the uncharacteristic afternoon autumn sunshine. After she'd thrown on some leggings and a tank top, Gemma went downstairs.

Looking out the kitchen window, she noticed Eric was back on the ladder, working on the shingles. She grabbed a tall glass from the cupboard, filled it with ice, and added some sweet tea with a slice of lemon. Then she made a thick ham sandwich with mustard and mayonnaise, just as Eric liked it. She put the sandwich on a plate, grabbed the glass of iced tea, and went outside.

"The boss says it's time for a break," she said with a smile, motioning him toward the picnic table under the tree.

"I'll clock out and be right there." He chuckled, climbing down the ladder.

Gemma sat on the bench, and Eric slid onto the one on the opposite side.

"This looks great. Thank you," he said as he took a huge gulp of the tea.

"You're welcome. Since you slept here last night, I realized you didn't bring any food with you today. Plus, it got really warm, and I figured you might be thirsty," she replied.

"Nothing for you?"

"Nah, I'm not too hungry, and I just had an iced coffee in town," Gemma answered.

"How did it go? I assume you met Agnes Daybell if you went to the historical society?" Eric asked between bites.

"Yeah, I did. She's a sweet old lady. She told me the people in town refer to the women in my family as the Jewels." She chuckled. "Did you know that?"

"I did. Your grandmother thought it was hilarious, and she played into it whenever she could." He laughed. "She was a character."

"Yeah, she was. I wish I had gotten to know her better." Gemma sighed.

"I know she wished that too," Eric told her.

"Anyway," she said, shaking off the sudden melancholy, "what do you know about the fires in Beacon Shores?"

"A bit." He shrugged. "What did you find out?"

"Well, I found out that Beacon Shores burned almost completely in 1899 and then again in 1905."

"That's true."

"Don't you find that odd? I mean, what are the chances of the same town burning down twice in just six years?" Gemma asked.

"It's definitely strange, but it happened," Eric replied with a shrug.

"Did they ever discover where the fires originated?"

"Not that I know of. But I don't really think it was ever investigated, at least not the way it would be now."

"Why wouldn't they have investigated it?"

"Probably because the townspeople had their own ideas about the fires, and they weren't interested in anything else."

"Their own ideas? What do you mean by that?"

"Emerald and I talked about this very same topic right before she passed away. She seemed to know you were going to ask this question, and she wanted to be sure she told me what she knew about it," Eric said.

"That's odd. How could she possibly know I'd ask the question?" Gemma chuckled.

"That's your grandmother for you, Gemma."

"Okay. Well, tell me what she said, then," she encouraged.

"Emerald told me that the real problems started in the winter of 1898," Eric began.

"What happened then?"

"It seemed that most of the people in Beacon Shores grew very ill. Emerald didn't know what sickness was being spread, but she said Pearl and her daughters were pretty much the only ones in town who didn't get sick," he said.

"That's odd, isn't it?" Gemma asked.

"Maybe. Maybe not. It honestly could have been anything. Maybe it was something Pearl and her daughters were already exposed and immune to. Who knows? But the people of Beacon Shores decided Pearl had caused the sickness."

Gemma scoffed. "Why would they think that? It's ridiculous."

"Pearl was well known as a healer. Most of the townspeople came to her on a regular basis for anything from gout and the common cold to childbirth and everything in between. She basically acted as the town's doctor, even though they already had one. People trusted her."

"So how did she go from being a beloved member of the community to the reason the town was sick?"

"I honestly don't know the answer to that, and neither did Emerald. All she knew was the people who had trusted Pearl and came to her for healing turned on her. They blamed her when the sickness hit the town. Probably because Pearl and her family didn't become ill. People weren't always rational back then, and they very rarely focused on science or facts," Eric explained.

"So, what happened then? What does this have to do with the fires?" Gemma questioned, trying to connect the pieces in her mind.

"Well, the good citizens of Beacon Shores decided then and there that Pearl was responsible, and therefore, she shouldn't be trusted."

"That's crazy."

"Crazy or not, that's the way it was. The town cut them off. They shunned Pearl and her daughters. They stopped coming to her for healing, they quit buying her tinctures, and the store stopped carrying her vegetables and jams. Pearl and her daughters became pariahs."

"That's terrible. They were all alone. I'm sure they depended on that income to survive," Gemma surmised. "What happened then?"

"Needless to say, it didn't go over well. Pearl was apparently an opinionated woman, and she didn't go down quietly."

"What did she do?"

"Rumor has it that she went into the town square and gave the good citizens a piece of her mind." Eric smirked.

"Meaning?"

"Meaning that Pearl Muller-Ackermann supposedly cursed the town of Beacon Shores."

"Cursed it?"

"Yep. She cursed it. So, when the town caught fire and burned just a few months later, you can probably guess who was to blame." Eric shrugged.

"Pearl."

"Bingo."

"Wow." Gemma sighed. "That's sort of a lot to digest, isn't it?"

"It is. And I truly have no idea how much fact there is to any of it. It's just the story your grandma Emerald told me."

"Well, thanks for telling me. It seems that each new piece of information I discover brings up about a thousand new questions that need answering." She laughed.

"You'll figure it out." He squeezed her hand. "I have no doubt that you'll piece this puzzle together eventually."

"I hope so."

"Anyway, I need to get back to work," Eric said, standing. "Thanks for lunch."

"You're welcome. Do you need any help with those shingles?"

"Nope. You need to get your cute little self up to

your room and work on your book," he answered with a laugh.

"No pressure, right?" She rolled her eyes as she grabbed the plate and cup and planted a quick kiss on Eric's cheek.

"No pressure at all, sweetheart." He smiled. "You've got this."

Twenty-Five

Gemma sat on the bed, her laptop, Pearl's journal, and the skeleton key spread out in front of her. She scrolled through the file she'd been working on, smiling when she saw the word count—over sixty thousand words—and realized her book was becoming a reality. In fact, it was nearly finished. Once she'd settled in on telling a fictionalized version of Pearl's story, the words had practically poured out of her.

Opening the journal, she flipped toward the end of it, noticing the date of the entry was December of 1898.

It's winter, and the cold dampness has settled in all around. The rain pours down on us, and the roar of the ocean howls just outside our back door. A strange sickness is spreading like wildfire through the town, my neighbors succumbing to it one by one. I don't know what's making them sick, but thanks be to God, my daughters and I seem to be immune. I believe it's because we live out here on our own, so far away from others. The people of Beacon Shores have their own ideas.

The mayor's wife paid me a visit today. It seems she believes that I'm to blame for the strange disease ravaging the town. She said my daughters and I will be on our own from now on. No one will visit us. No one will buy our wares. No one will seek me out for healing. We are not welcome to come into town. They believe I've caused this sickness, bringing it to life and spreading it through my supposed association with the Evil One. If only they understood that my heart is true. I serve God and God only.

The mayor's wife told me the banishment will end when I release the spell I've cast upon the people of Beacon Shores. But since I've cast no spell, I cannot release it. My daughters will suffer because of me. If only I knew a way to fix this! I became so angry, my rage bubbling inside me like a stew. It was sinful to be so vexed, but I couldn't help myself.

"This town will pay for what it has done to my family. Curses upon you all!"

I yelled this at the mayor's wife before slamming the door in her face. And then, before I gave myself the chance to calm down, I went into the town square and said it again.

God forgive me.

Gemma wiped the tears from her eyes as she finished reading Pearl's journal entry. She could almost feel Pearl's sadness and desperation jump through the pages, through the years. What kind of crazy superstition would cause an entire town to shun a family because they believed they had supernaturally caused some sort of epidemic?

Flipping a couple pages ahead, Gemma looked closely at the words, her forehead wrinkling in confusion. The entry was dated spring of 1899.

"The handwriting is different," she whispered.

Gemma turned back to the first page of the journal and compared all the writing from the beginning up to that point. The rest of the entries were clearly penned by a different hand. Heart pounding inside her chest, she began to read.

My mama is gone.

My mama is gone.

No matter how many times I say the words out loud, I don't believe them. Maybe writing them down will make them seem more real. I don't know how to live in a world without my mother, and I don't know if I want to learn.

Her last words to me were "Amie, you are strong. You must be strong for Ru. My girls. I'll be with you forever." And then she was gone, taken away by those angry men.

When they came to Moonstone House in the middle of the night, I thought I was dreaming. When they banged on our door and called us out while we were sleeping in our beds, I didn't think it was really happening. But when Ru and I followed Mama outside on the front porch and the men grabbed her, I understood it was a nightmare come to life. They screamed that it was Mama's fault the town had burned. It was because of her curse.

So they tied her hands and feet and placed a noose around her neck. Ru and I screamed and cried, but no one could hear us over the mob screaming, "Hang the witch." They acted as if we weren't even there, as if they hadn't stolen our mother from us right before our eyes. Fearing for myself and Ru, I grabbed her, and we ran. We hid in the woods beside the house.

When the sun finally came up the next morning, the chaos and yelling had stopped. I grabbed Ru's trembling hand, and we walked toward the house. We both screamed when we saw her there. Those men took my mother and hanged her from the lowest branch of the redbud tree. Every flower on the tree had fallen off, scattered like the broken pieces of our hearts, littering the ground below. My mother and the tree, their connection so strong, both died together.

Ru and I cried for hours, sobbing until the deep well of our tears finally ran dry. I looked at her body, still hanging in the tree, but I knew her soul had gone home. My mother was with God. Now it was my job to carry on. I was eighteen, and Ru was nine, but I had to be her mother now.

Ru and I gently took Mama's body from the branch, carefully handling her, giving her all the love we could in that final moment. We dug a deep hole next to the redbud tree, each of us taking turns with the shovel. Together, Ru and I placed our mother's body inside and covered it with dirt.

I looked at the empty branches of the redbud tree, once so glorious. Ru and I gathered all the fallen flowers and piled them on top of our mother's newly dug grave. It was as if the tree couldn't handle being in the world without her. I didn't know if I could either.

I had watched my mother grow that tree from nothing but a couple seeds and her words. It was her tree, and if I couldn't have her in the world, I wanted the redbud tree.

"Herr Jesu dir leb ich, Herr Jesu dir sterb ich, Herr Jesu dein bin ich todt un lebendig... Lord Jesus, I live to thee, Lord Jesus, I die to thee, Lord Jesus, I am thine, in death and in life," I murmured quietly, remembering the words my mother had spoken the day she grew the tree.

Ru grabbed my hand, and I said the words twice more.

"In the name of the Father, the Son, and the Holy Spirit, Amen," I finished.

Ru and I both crossed ourselves.

Nodding toward Ru, I said, "Now. It's time."

Ru took a deep breath, closed her eyes, and began to sing.

"Listen close and you'll find me,
Buried 'neath the Remembering Tree.
Tucked inside and nestled deep,
Buried 'neath the Remembering Tree.

Hearts of hatred, hearts of greed
Seek the treasure buried deep.
Only she who holds the key
Will unearth the secrets of the Remembering Tree."

When Ru finished singing, we stood there, my sister and me, hand in hand, watching, waiting. I heard the first tiny popping sound, and then hundreds more followed as the buds blossomed and sprang to life. The tree was no longer bare. The branches were alive once again, resplendent with lush red flowers.

"The Remembering Tree will bloom forever, a reminder of what happened here. We will never forget the wrong that was done to our family. This is for you, Mama," I whispered, wiping the tears from my eyes.

Gemma let out the breath she didn't even know she'd been holding. She grabbed a tissue from the bedside table and blew her nose and wiped her eyes. Her heart actually hurt inside for what she'd just read. Pearl had been murdered, hanged from the redbud tree while her daughters watched.

And the song the younger girl had sung was the same one that haunted Gemma.

There were so many questions to answer, so many things she needed to know. With a heavy heart, Gemma closed the journal and returned it to the dresser drawer.

~

Later that evening, Eric and Gemma sat at the dining room table sharing a pizza. Neither had felt like cooking, and both had been famished after the long day. Abigail had asked Gemma if she wanted Opal to stay with them a little longer, and Gemma had agreed. It still didn't feel safe at Moonstone House, and the more she learned about the dark history of what had happened there, the less secure she felt.

As much as she missed her, Gemma was relieved that Opal was staying with Abigail. They'd spoken on the phone several times throughout the day, and although Opal wanted to be at home, she had agreed to stay put until they figured out what was going on.

"How did the writing go this afternoon?" Eric asked between bites.

"I didn't get many words written," Gemma answered.

"That's okay. It'll come," he encouraged.

"I got a little sidetracked by the journal today, I guess."

"Did you find out new information?"

"Yeah, I did. And I guess I'm still trying to process it. It's really sad, Eric," Gemma said, her eyes filling with tears.

"Can you tell me about it?"

"I suppose so," she began. "The whole journal, up to the point I read today, was written by Pearl. I guess I just thought she'd written the entire thing, but I was wrong."

"Someone else wrote in Pearl's journal?"

"Yep. In spring of 1899, the author of the journal switches from Pearl to her oldest daughter, Amie," she told him.

"Why is that?"

Gemma took a deep breath and tried to force the words that were so difficult to speak. "Amie started writing in the journal after Pearl died."

"I see."

"Eric, Pearl was murdered. A band of men, presumably led by Dogan Becker, came to Moonstone House in the middle of the night, tied her up, and hanged her from the redbud tree," she cried. "In front of her daughters!"

"I'm so sorry you had to read that, Gemma," he said, grabbing her hand and squeezing it. "It's awful."

"How can people be so cruel? How could they hang her from the tree in her own yard while her children watched? How could they blame her because the town got sick? Did they really think she was the reason the town burned?"

Gemma buried her head in her hands and sobbed. She felt such a strong connection to Pearl, and learning what had happened to her was soul-crushing.

"People have always feared what they don't understand, pretty much since the beginning of time. And that fear causes some people to do unspeakable things," Eric said quietly.

She wiped her face and tried to control her tears. "I just can't believe it. I can't believe that happened here... at Moonstone House... to my great-great-grandmother."

"The women in your family are special, Gemma. They're smart, strong, resourceful, and resilient. It's no wonder weaker men fear them," he told her. "That doesn't excuse it, but I think it explains it."

"And it's happening again. To me," she said quietly.

"Gemma, I will not let anyone hurt you," Eric said forcefully. "I swear I won't."

"And I believe you. But it's not even the fact that I'm afraid," she began.

"What else is bothering you?"

"It's just... I feel like... like I have a job to do. Like it's my place to do something. I feel like it's up to me to end this thing, once and for all."

"How are you going to do that?"

"I have no idea. But I'm going to figure it out, I can promise you that. Sooner or later, all the pieces of this puzzle are going to come together. And when that happens, I'll know what to do," Gemma replied, standing up to clear the dishes.

Eric rose to assist her. "I hope you'll let me help you when the time comes. You don't have to take this on alone."

"I know. And I really appreciate that. More than you know."

She placed the dishes in the sink and turned toward him. She pulled him close and wrapped her arms around him, sinking deep into his embrace. Turning her face up to his, she stood on her toes and kissed his lips softly.

The kiss grew in intensity, the spark lighting a flame that burned into a blazing wildfire. When she came up for air, she looked into Eric's eyes, seeing herself reflected there so completely that it took her breath away.

"Stay with me tonight, Eric," she whispered.

"I told you I'll be here," he answered.

"I mean stay with me... next to me. Not on the couch. Spend tonight beside me."

Before she could speak another word, his mouth overtook hers, and nothing else in the whole world mattered.

Twenty-Six

"Okay, honey, I love you too," Gemma said to Opal on the phone. "Yes, you can come home soon. I just want to be sure you're safe. I know. Have a good day at school, and call me when you get back to Ryder's house."

Hanging up the phone, she sighed heavily. She hated the fact that her daughter wasn't at home where she belonged. She wanted her there more than anything. But something, some instinct deep inside her gut, told her that Moonstone House wasn't the safest place for Opal. She had to listen to her intuition. If something were to happen to her daughter, and she could have prevented it, she'd never forgive herself.

Gemma looked out the kitchen window and saw Eric working in the yard. She smiled, thinking back to the night before. Being with him had been everything she'd imagined it would be, and although she'd wondered if she would regret their intimacy afterward, there wasn't a single part of her that would change a thing. They felt right together, a perfect combination of friendship and passion, and she wouldn't take it back even if she could.

Pouring herself another cup of coffee, Gemma grabbed her mug and went upstairs to her room. Placing the mug on the bedside table, she opened her laptop. Then she went to the dresser drawer and looked inside. Normally, she just worked with the journal, but that day, she also grabbed the old copy of the German book, *Der Lange Verborgene Freund*.

Plopping down on the bed, she opened her web browser. Mentally crossing her fingers, she typed in the name of the old book, hoping to find the translation. A quick glance at the search results gave her the answer. It was written by a man named John George Hohman, and it was thought to be a sort of magical book, giving the owner supposed protection. The translation told her the book was called *Long Hidden Friend* or *Long Lost Friend*. It was a book of charms used by Brauchers to fend off illness and give protection, covering everything from sick livestock to warding off evil.

"What an interesting woman you were, Pearl Muller-Ackermann," Gemma said quietly. "You continue to astound me."

She flipped through the pages of *Der Lange Verborgene Freund,* realizing the entire book was written in German. She couldn't read it. Short of typing it word for word into the translation tool, or finding someone who spoke German, she would have no clue what it said. Sighing, she thumbed through the pages anyway. As she did, an old, faded, time-weathered piece of paper fell out of the book.

"What's this?" Gemma asked, carefully unfolding it.

Looking closely at the paper, she recognized the handwriting immediately. It was Pearl's. Taking a deep breath, she slowly read the page, thankfully written in English.

AGAINST EVIL SPIRITS AND ALL MANNER OF WITCHCRAFT

All this be guarded here in time, and there in eternity. Amen

Our Braucherei tradition is based on the fact that we love and believe in God with our whole hearts. That is the very basis of our beliefs. But within our tradition, there may also come a suspicion of witchcraft. It is believed that some Brauchers, those seeking greater power, make pacts with the Devil. When this happens, the curse of witchcraft is given by the Evil One. This curse forces the Braucher to work nefarious spells against others for as long as he lives.

Once the curse of witchcraft is placed upon the Braucher, he must comply. If he refuses to comply, he may become ill and quite possibly die. If he dies, his soul will be stuck in limbo, unable to cross over. In order to be free, the Braucher must first pass on the curse of witchcraft to one of his descendants so he may find rest in the afterlife. This is the price that must be paid for such power.

Wrinkling her forehead, Gemma read the words once again. Trying to make sense of it, she focused in as they jumped off the page at her—witchcraft, curse, power, Devil, limbo, descendants.

"So, if a Braucher decides he wants more power, he might turn to witchcraft," she mused to herself. "And in order to avoid being stuck in limbo after his death, he has to pass his curse on to his descendants."

Gemma chewed on her lip, concentrating. Something was there, some piece of the puzzle just waiting to be discovered. She read Pearl's words over again, trying her best to make the connection in her brain. The thought began as a small inkling, then grew to a possibility. The words leaped off the page as she thought back on all she'd seen and read since coming to Moonstone House.

Was it possible?

It barely made sense to her, and yet the idea was tunneling its way through her brain. What if Dogan Becker had also been a practitioner of the Braucherei tradition? What if he had wanted to be more powerful, and in order to obtain that power, he had turned to witchcraft? What if he had passed on the curse to his descendants, like Dominic, so he wouldn't be stuck in limbo?

Wouldn't that be the epitome of hypocrisy—to hang Pearl as a witch when he was one himself?

It all seemed too far-fetched to even be likely, but she was learning that nothing was impossible at Moonstone House.

"Keep digging, Gemma. You're going to figure it out," she murmured to herself.

Twenty-Seven

By the time Eric finished with work that afternoon, Gemma had made up her mind. She was determined to get to the bottom of what had been going on at Moonstone House for generations, and it hit her like a lightning bolt that she had her own special ace in the hole—Eric.

The thought occurred to her earlier in the day, and she'd been stewing on it ever since. She found herself wishing she could sit down and have a conversation with Grandma Emerald about everything that had happened. That was when she realized that maybe she could, at least with his help. She just had to figure out the right way to ask him. She honestly had no clue how the whole talking to the dead thing actually worked.

"Hi there," Eric said as he pulled her close and kissed her.

"Hi yourself," she replied when her lips were free. "How was work?"

"Good. I accomplished everything on my list for the day. The shingles are replaced on the outbuilding, and the barn is all painted except for one side."

"Very productive." She nodded.

"I've got to say that I'm loving the commute." He chuckled, grabbing a can of Coke from the refrigerator and chugging it down. "I just wake up and walk outside."

"Not bad at all." She laughed. "Just think of the gas money you're saving."

"Yeah, the company isn't too bad either," he added with a laugh.

"My sentiments exactly."

"I was thinking that maybe we should go into town and have dinner tonight. What do you say?" Eric inquired.

"Well, that sounds lovely and quite nice," she offered.

"I'm sensing a 'but.'" He laughed.

"But I actually had something else in mind," Gemma began, preparing herself for what she was about to say.

"Okay, no problem. What do you want to do?"

"There's something I really want. But I don't know if it's possible."

"Well, there's only one way to find out. Lay it on me," he said as he walked into the living room and plopped down on the couch cushion.

"All right," she started, sitting beside him. "I guess I'll just say it, then."

She chewed nervously at the skin on the sides of her nails.

"You're not saying anything." Eric chuckled.

"Ugh, I feel like I'm going to sound stupid." Gemma sighed.

"Babe, just say it. Tell me what's on your mind."

"Okay, you asked for it." She took a deep breath. "I want to talk to Grandma Emerald."

"Hmmm, well, I have to say I didn't see that one coming."

Eric placed his empty soda can on the coffee table and leaned forward, rubbing his chin thoughtfully.

"See, it's stupid, right?" Gemma slumped back on the couch. "And probably impossible."

"No, it's not stupid. And yes, we can try." He sat up a little straighter and faced her.

"Really? I can talk to her?" Gemma leaned forward excitedly.

"I said we can try," he explained. "I never really know what's going to happen, Gemma. Generally, when I see your grandmother, she just sort of shows up. I don't usually summon her, so to speak."

"But you can, right?" she asked. "I mean, you're able to do that. You did it with Clayton."

"Sometimes it works. And I can see it's important to you, so I'll do my best." He shrugged.

"That's all I'm asking. Just try. If it doesn't work, then I'll know it wasn't meant to be," Gemma agreed. "But if it does work, she might be able to answer the questions I have."

"Deal."

"So, how does it happen? Is there some sort of ceremony or something?"

"That's not really how I do things." He cleared his throat. "I don't have a specific ritual or anything like that. I just send her a message, and then I wait to see if she receives it."

"And if she does—receive it, I mean—then I can talk to her?"

"You're probably not going to hear her voice, sweetheart. If that's what you're hoping for, you will most likely be disappointed. How it works is that you'll speak, and then she'll answer through me," Eric explained.

"But I've heard her voice already. Since I've been here at Moonstone House, I mean," Gemma revealed.

"You have?"

"Yeah, a couple times. Right when I first arrived. I was feeling pretty low, and I felt her in the room with me. I heard her speak to me."

"That's pretty amazing. Maybe you will be able to hear her, then. I guess we'll just have to see what happens."

"Can we do it now?" she asked, excited to find the answers.

"Sure." He smiled.

Eric closed his eyes, and Gemma watched as he grew very still and silent. She noticed his breathing slowing measurably, his chest expanding and contracting in a steady rhythm. An array of expressions passed over his face, and she wished she could see what he saw and experience what this felt like for him. He sat like that, almost perfectly still, for about five minutes. Gemma barely moved, barely breathed, for fear of disrupting the moment.

All at once, Eric's eyes fluttered open, and he focused them on her. "She's here. Your grandmother is here."

"Grandma?" Gemma's voice quivered.

"She's with you, Gemma. You can talk to her. She says hello."

"You were right. I can't hear her voice."

"It's all right. She'll speak through me. Just say what you want to say."

"I, uh... hi there, um, Grandma," she began, suddenly unsure of herself. "I've been reading Pearl's journal. I'm guessing you already knew that."

"She says she knew you would find it," Eric channeled. "She always believed you would be the one who would end this. She says she saw the gifts in you when you were a little girl."

"Gifts?"

"She says you have the gift of keen observation, the gift of deep understanding, the ability to find hidden truths. That's what you're going to need in order to put an end to this."

"I'm trying. I'm really trying," Gemma replied. "There's just so much I still don't understand."

"She says you're on the right path. Ask her what you want to know. She'll tell you what she can."

"Just like that? Um, okay. Well, the first question I have is this: What can you tell me about Dogan Becker?"

"He cannot be trusted. It may seem he's dead and gone, but he is very much alive and well."

"He's alive? Do you mean that metaphorically? He's not, like, actually alive, right?"

"She says you can't underestimate him."

"Okay," Gemma agreed, nodding. "Next question: Was Dogan Becker a Braucher?"

"Emerald says you've discovered the heart of the matter. Yes, he was."

"I knew it," Gemma said vehemently. "Then why did Dogan hate Pearl so much? If they both came from similar backgrounds and traditions, wouldn't they have gotten along better? Like, joined forces or something? I mean, they're both in the same small community, in a remote coastal region in the state of Washington. They both practiced an obscure tradition from the Pennsylvania Dutch culture. I can't understand why they wouldn't have banded together."

Eric's forehead wrinkled, and he closed his eyes tightly for a moment. After a slight pause, he opened them once again and spoke.

"The Braucherei practice is very territorial. When a Braucher comes to an area, it is understood and agreed upon that he or she will be the only healer in that area. Brauchers do not share their territories."

"So Dogan didn't like it when Pearl came to Beacon Shores?" Gemma asked.

"Emerald says it was the opposite. Pearl was here

first. She was the practicing Braucher. Dogan came to Beacon Shores a few years after Pearl. He was wealthy. He became the mayor. He believed he was more important, especially because he was a man and she was a woman. He also feared Pearl's power. He told her she must stop practicing."

"What? He came to Beacon Shores and tried to push her out?"

"Pearl refused to back down. She had been here first, establishing herself as a healer. People trusted her. She believed it was her calling."

"I can't imagine that made Dogan Becker very happy," Gemma mused.

"When Pearl refused to stop her practice, Dogan proceeded to turn the town against her. He kept his own Braucherei practice a secret from everyone but Pearl, and his entire life's mission centered on destroying her. He convinced the town that she was a witch, the one to blame for the epidemic that winter, as well as the fire that came after. He eventually led the mob that ended Pearl's life."

Gemma let the information trickle into her brain, the pieces beginning to click together. Dogan wanted Pearl to do his bidding, to bow to his authority, and when she refused, he set out to destroy her. Anger bubbled up from somewhere deep inside Gemma, a primal, primitive sort of rage that she'd never felt before. It was almost as if she were experiencing a genetic memory of the ordeal.

Gathering her wits about her, she said, "I want to know why Dominic Becker wants Moonstone House. What's in it for him?"

Eric paused a moment, seemingly collecting his own thoughts. "She says Dominic is here to finish what Dogan started."

"He wants to take me down," Gemma stated.

"Emerald wants me to tell you that you need to do some more research."

"Research on what?"

"You need to educate yourself on how to remove a witchcraft curse," Eric channeled.

"How am I supposed to do that?" Gemma tried to hold back the exasperation in her voice, but it was no use.

"Your grandmother says you need to find a Braucher. She says they still exist."

"You want me to hunt down a modern-day Braucher, Grandma? I think that's going to be a little harder than you think," Gemma said, a bit derisively.

Eric remained quiet for a full minute, then shook his head lightly and blinked twice. "She's gone."

Twenty-Eight

Two more weeks came and went, and Gemma was still working to piece together the puzzle of the past. Opal had been back home several times, to hang out with her mother and to pick up more clothes, but they had all decided she was much safer in town for the time being.

Gemma's determination grew by the day. The fact that it didn't feel safe to have her daughter in her own home only fueled her fire. She'd been studying, searching for answers, and she'd compiled an impressive body of work. She had learned a lot, but there were still way too many things left unanswered.

The police had allegedly questioned Dominic Becker, but just as Gemma predicted, they had come up empty. Dominic apparently had an airtight alibi for the evening, and given his position of power, and the fact that his money spoke volumes, the investigation had gone no further. The police told her they were sorry, but as far as they were concerned, the incident was probably caused by some teenagers getting too rowdy, just some harmless fun that spiraled out of control.

Gemma knew better. Deep in her core she knew that both of the supposed "pranks" were warnings of something far more dangerous to come. She had to figure out the answer, to stop whatever was coming before it could hurt her family any more than it had already.

She pulled out her laptop and opened her email, praying she'd received the response she'd been waiting for. Just as Emerald had instructed, Gemma had looked for a Braucher. She'd been skeptical about finding someone, but a Google search had turned up the name of a man living in Pennsylvania claiming to be a modern-day Braucher.

His name was Rowan Powell. She had emailed him, giving a precursory explanation of what she was looking for, and she'd received an "out of the office" automatic response. According to the email, he was out of town for two weeks, but each and every day, she opened her messages, hoping to see a reply. Taking a deep breath, she opened her email program and smiled when she saw his name in her inbox.

She read through the message quickly, happy that he was willing to speak with her. He even gave her his personal phone number. Pennsylvania was three hours ahead of Washington, but a quick glance at her watch told Gemma that it was still an appropriate time to make the call. Punching in the digits, she waited for him to pick up the phone.

When he answered, she introduced herself, exchanged the basic pleasantries, and then begged for his help. Rowan seemed happy and interested in giving it to her. She explained a bit of background on her situation, and he offered up some more history on the Braucherei traditions. A lot of what he told her she had learned herself over the past couple weeks. She had totally and completely immersed herself in learning everything she could about the practice.

"So, Rowan, what can you tell me about breaking a witchcraft curse?" Gemma inquired.

"Breaking curses is tricky business, but it can be done," Rowan replied.

"How would one go about doing such a thing?"

"The easiest way is for the afflicted family member to be ready and willing to get rid of the evil power," he answered.

Gemma thought about the Becker family's obsession with power, and she knew without a doubt that Dominic wasn't going to give up that power willingly. If, in fact, he had been given the witchcraft curse to begin with, Dominic Becker would hold on to it to the bitter end.

"Well, what if cooperation isn't a possibility? I mean, what if the person doesn't want to give up the power? What if he's desperate to hold on to it? Can someone sort of, I don't know, take it away from him?"

"I'm not going to lie to you. That's very difficult, Gemma." Rowan sighed.

"Difficult, but not impossible?" she asked hopefully.

"Not entirely impossible, I suppose," he conceded.

"How would one go about doing such a thing?"

"In the case of a witchcraft curse, the original Braucher would have needed to pass on his curse to a descendant in order to cross over into the afterlife. If this curse had been handed down through the generations, then the modern-day descendant would still have the original Braucher's spell book," Rowan revealed.

"You're serious?"

"I am."

"Okay." Gemma sighed. "What else?"

"If you're set on breaking the witchcraft curse, you're going to need to get your hands on the original spell book."

"Wow. Okay. That seems... difficult."

"Well, brace yourself, because it's about to get even harder, Gemma. You see, in order to break the curse, you need to take the original spell book, with a lock of hair from the original Braucher, and bury it six feet in the ground," Rowan revealed.

"How am I supposed to get a lock of hair from Dogan Becker? He's been dead and buried for over a hundred years."

"I have no idea. I'm telling you this only in theory. I've never seen it done in practice," he admitted.

Gemma tapped her ink pen on her chin, a thousand thoughts circulating through her muddled brain. What Rowan was saying seemed impossible. How on earth was she supposed to get a lock of Dogan's hair? Dig up his grave and hope there was some growing on his corpse?

"Wait a minute," she began as an idea popped into her head. "The original Braucher's descendants would share his DNA. If I were able to get a lock of hair from his descendant, would that serve the same purpose?"

Getting a lock of Dominic's hair was going to be

anything but simple, but it was a whole lot more reasonable than trying to figure out how to get Dogan's.

"Well, I don't know, honestly," he replied. "It's possible that it might work, but I couldn't say one way or another. There are no guarantees."

"Okay." Gemma sighed.

She had known that the act of breaking a generational curse wasn't going to be a walk in the park, but she hadn't imagined it would require something like what Rowan was suggesting.

"Thank you so much for your help, Rowan. You don't know how much I appreciate you sharing your knowledge with me."

"It's truly my pleasure, Gemma. I'm always happy to keep the traditions alive and introduce them to those who show an interest."

"Before I let you go, I have one last question," she said.

"What's that?"

"Do you have any idea where I might begin to search for an original spell book?"

"If what you say is true and a witchcraft curse has been passed down through a family, then the original spell book would have to exist. And if it does, it will be kept close to the modern-day descendant. He'll use it frequently," Rowan explained.

Gemma thanked him once again and hung up the phone. Drumming her fingers on the table, she began to formulate a plan.

"Watch out, Dominic Becker, because I'm coming for you."

Twenty-Nine

Later that evening, Gemma and Eric sat on the couch, snuggled together in front of the crackling fireplace. The evenings had grown cold, and she thought a fire was a cozy way to wind down for the night. Eric seemed relaxed for the first time in days, and she almost reconsidered the conversation she wanted to have with him but then thought better of it. The sooner she could put her plan into action, the sooner they could get back to normal life.

"So, there's something I wanted to talk to you about," Gemma began, pulling her head off his chest and sitting up straight.

"Sure thing. You know you can talk to me about anything." He smiled.

"Do you remember when Emerald said I needed to

find a modern-day Braucher? To find out how to break a witchcraft curse?"

"Yep, I remember. That's hard to forget. What about it?"

"Well." She took a deep breath. "I found one. His name is Rowan Powell, and he lives in Pennsylvania. He's a Braucher, and he told me what I need to do in order to break this curse."

"Wow. Okay." Eric ran his fingers through his hair, a sign that Gemma had learned to associate with nervousness. "What did he say?"

"Well, it's not going to be easy, but it's not impossible."

"I can't imagine you believe anything is impossible, babe. That's one of the things I admire most about you."

"Great. I'm glad you agree. So, all I need to do is get my hands on Dogan's original spell book, which Rowan says will be in Dominic's possession. I also need to get a lock of Dominic's hair and bury it six feet in the ground along with the spell book. Rowan says that will probably break the curse."

She rattled off the words quickly, needing to say them before she lost her nerve.

"Wait a minute, what?"

Eric sat up straighter. Gemma could see she had his full attention.

"I know, I know, it sounds crazy, but I really believe it will work."

"Gemma, come on. Do you think Dominic is just going to hand over the spell book and a chunk of his hair to you?" He laughed derisively. "That's not going to happen."

"No, of course I don't think that." She shook her head. "But I have a plan."

"I'm sure you do."

"Just listen a minute. I'm going to contact Dominic. I'll tell him I've reconsidered and that I want to meet at his house to talk to him about buying Moonstone House. Once I'm there, I'm going to look around and find Dogan's spell book. I'm sure there's a hairbrush lying around somewhere, so that solves that lock of hair problem," Gemma explained.

"Have you lost your mind?" Eric jumped from the couch and began to pace back and forth across the living room floor.

"No, I haven't," she replied in a clipped tone. "I'm being totally and completely serious here."

"Do you have any idea how dangerous Dominic Becker is, Gemma? He's given you two warnings already.

The next time is going to be way more serious. And you want to walk right into the lion's den and invite him to attack you? I can't believe I'm hearing this."

Eric's face grew redder by the minute, and Gemma believed his head might actually explode at any second. She didn't think he would be in love with her idea, but she hadn't anticipated a reaction like that.

Taking a deep breath, Gemma stood and walked across the room. She positioned her body in front of his, forcing him to stop pacing, and placed her hands on both of his arms.

"Hey, stop for a minute. I need you to breathe, Eric. You look like you're about to combust," she said.

"That's because I am. Please tell me you're not serious." He looked at her, his blue eyes pleading.

"Look, I know you don't like the idea, but yes, I'm serious. I've been looking for a way to end this, and now I finally know what it is. I know how to do it."

"But it's too dangerous! Dominic Becker is after you. He wants to take you down. You cannot willingly place yourself in his path."

"If I want to finish this, that's exactly what I have to do, Eric."

"Well, I won't let you!" He pulled away from her and stalked into the kitchen.

Gemma was pinioned in place, unable to move.

The force of his anger was shocking. She'd never seen that side of Eric. In fact, she would have never believed he had it in him to be that mad.

She waited a couple minutes, hoping to give him time to calm down, and then she went into the kitchen.

He was bent over the counter, his head in his hands. When he heard her come in, he lifted his face and looked at her. The pain she saw there was excruciating.

"I'm sorry," he said. "I didn't mean to raise my voice to you."

"I know. I'm sorry I just threw that at you," she replied. "I could have at least eased into it."

"Babe, there isn't any amount of easing that's going to make that idea palatable for me."

"It's not like I have a lot of choices here. I mean, I'm lucky I found one way to break a curse. I'm guessing there aren't a lot of other options out there."

"I know," he said. "So let me do it."

"Do what?"

"Let me get the book from Dominic."

Gemma's eyes widened. "Are you kidding me? He'd be on to you in a second. You'd kill each other."

"I could do it," he insisted. "I could control myself."

"No, I don't think you could. As much as you want to be the one, this is up to me. This is my quest, so to speak."

"I can't stand the thought of him hurting you. I can't bear to think of you in danger."

"I know."

"I don't think you do, Gemma. Not really."

"Then explain it to me. Why is it so hard for you to let me do this?"

Eric walked around the counter and stood in front of her. He reached down and tipped her face up toward his. "Because I've fallen in love with you, Gemma. I am totally and completely in love with you. I've been waiting for you for so long, and the thought of anyone hurting you makes me want to put my fist through the wall."

"You love me?" Her voice trembled.

"Oh yeah, I sure do. I think I fell the minute you stepped out of your car that very first day. Maybe even before. I feel like I've loved you my entire lifetime and several others that came before that."

"Is that even possible?" Gemma asked quietly, her heart swelling inside her chest.

"Anything is possible. Haven't you figured that out by now?"

"It sure feels that way when I'm with you."

"Gemma, the thought of you putting yourself in danger is a no-go for me. We'll have to find another way."

"I'm still stuck on the fact that you just told me you love me." She smiled.

"Does that surprise you? It shouldn't. I've loved you for a hundred years."

"A hundred years, huh? Isn't that an exaggeration?"

"Nope. Not even a little bit." He smiled mysteriously.

"Hearing you say the words makes it real."

"I guess it does."

"I do too, you know," she said quietly.

"What?" He grinned.

"I love you too."

THIRTY

Gemma rolled over slowly, trying her best not to wake Eric. He had fallen asleep next to her, and she wanted to keep it that way. He needed to rest. He'd gotten so worked up earlier when she'd shared her plan. She knew he was exhausted from work, not to mention the fact that he'd been sleeping on her couch in order to keep her safe. The last thing she wanted was to disturb his peaceful slumber.

Gemma propped herself up on her elbow and watched him as moonlight trickled in through the window. His face was almost angelic in repose. He also didn't snore, which was an added bonus. She had fallen pretty hard for Eric Johnson.

Gently, she brushed a strand of wayward hair from his forehead and sighed. She knew she had to at least try her plan. It was the only way. After seeing Eric's reaction to it, she also understood she was going to have to do it without his knowledge.

She didn't have a clue how she was going to pull that off, seeing as how they were basically joined at the hip these days, but she was going to have to figure it out. If it was even remotely possible that she could break the witchcraft curse, she was going to give it a shot.

The next morning, Gemma woke, finding herself alone. She glanced at the bedside clock, shocked to see it was almost ten o'clock. She hadn't slept that late in ages! Rolling out of bed, she threw on jeans and a sweatshirt, spritzed some water on her curls to refresh them, and went downstairs.

Eric had brewed a pot of coffee, so she poured some into her favorite mug and headed outside to find him. He was at the barn. He had just finished painting the final side, and it looked wonderful.

"Hey there," she said. "I woke up, and you were gone. I didn't like it."

"I was wide awake at five o'clock, and you were out like a light, so I wasn't about to wake you," he replied.

"You're done with the barn."

"I am."

"I can't believe all the changes you've made around here." She glanced around the yard, taking in all the repairs and renovations he'd finished in the past months.

"It's been a joint effort."

"True. But it was mostly you," she pointed out.

"Well, I think we should just stick to the fact that we make a great team," he added.

"Okay. Deal."

"So, I have to go out of town today," Eric began.

"Out of town? Where? For how long?"

"As soon as I change my clothes, I have to drive over to Deep River. The panes for the broken window came in. I ordered them last week, and they weren't supposed to arrive until Saturday, but they called and said they got there early."

"Oh, that's great. I am definitely ready to get the plywood off the window," she said. "How far away is Deep River?"

"It's about a three-hour drive. I'll be home tonight, but it'll be late. I was thinking maybe you'd want to ride along with me?"

"That sounds nice, but I promised Opal I'd bring her some more clothes this afternoon and grab her dirty laundry. I also want to visit with her for a while. I miss her."

"I understand. Well, then, maybe you should ask Abigail if you can stay there instead of coming back home?" he suggested. "I don't like the thought of you being here alone right now."

"It's very sweet of you to worry, but I'm not about to do that." She shook her head.

"C'mon. Do it for me. Please?"

"I love you, but no. I'm going to take Opal's things to her, and then I'll just be here working on the book. I'm almost done, and I plan to use every spare moment to finish it. But I'll make sure I keep all the doors and windows locked, and my phone will be next to me every second."

"Gemma—"

"Nope. You're going to have to back down on this one. I want to be here, inside my own house. I refuse to be pushed out of it. Even by you." She smiled sweetly.

He sighed heavily, and Gemma was sure he was going to argue. But he didn't. "Fine. You are a stubborn woman, but I get it. This is your home, and no one should make you leave it. Not even me."

"Thank you for understanding." She popped onto her toes and gave him a quick peck on the cheek.

"I don't like it, but I'm not going to push. Just promise me you'll be careful."

"I'll be careful."

Thirty-One

Gemma sighed as Eric's truck pulled out of the driveway. She hated the fact that she hadn't been completely honest with him, but there was no other way. She'd been worried about how she was going to put her plan into action, but as soon as Eric told her he had to go to Deep River and wouldn't be back until late that night, she had taken it as a sign.

Grabbing her phone, she looked at Dominic's business card, thankful she'd kept it instead of ripping it up like she'd wanted to. Punching the digits into the phone, she waited as it rang twice. On the third one, he picked up.

"Hello."

The sound of his voice made her feel like she was

going to vomit. She was tempted to hang up before she could say what she'd planned to, but she forced herself to answer him.

"Hello, Dominic. This is Gemma Clayborn."

"Gemma, what a nice surprise! I didn't think I'd be hearing from you," he practically purred.

"Well, I've had some time to think about your offer, and I'd like to let you know that I've reconsidered," she said, nausea rippling in her stomach.

"You have? Well, now, that is shocking. You were so adamant about wanting to keep Moonstone House in the family."

"Well, Dominic, money talks, as they say. I consider myself a smart woman, and the thought of you making me rich sounds pretty good right about now." She forced herself to laugh.

"Oh, I can definitely make you rich."

"Perfect. Let's get together and talk about that, then. What do you say?"

"I say I'll be at your place in thirty minutes," he replied quickly.

"No. Not here. I, uh... well I haven't really told my daughter about this yet. I want to hear what you have to say first," she lied.

"I understand completely. You'll come here, then.

I'll have my chef make us dinner. How does six o'clock sound to you? I'll send a car."

"No, no, I'll drive myself," she insisted.

"Very well. I'll see you at my house this evening, then."

"Sounds like a plan."

Gemma hung up the phone, shoved her shaking hands into the pockets of her jeans, and told herself to breathe.

"All right," she said to herself. "It looks like I just made a deal with the devil."

Thirty-Two

Gemma pulled her car into the circular driveway of Dominic's massive home. The immense stone mansion looked more like a castle than a house. It was cold and intimidating, a bit like Dominic himself. Wiping her sweaty palms on her skirt, she applied another layer of red lipstick, fluffed her hair, slid out of the car, and shut the door.

She'd taken extra time on her appearance that evening, choosing a black formfitting pencil skirt, her highest black heels, and a sleek, red, low-cut blouse that accentuated her petite shape in all the right places. She wasn't a shallow woman, but she also wasn't above using every tool at her disposal in order to land her intended target. Men were visual creatures, so she planned to give Dominic something to look at.

She was about to ring the bell when a man in a tuxedo opened the door.

"Ms. Clayborn, I presume," he said in a British accent.

"Oh, uh... yeah. Gemma, call me Gemma," she stammered, caught off guard.

"Mr. Becker is waiting for you on the veranda. Follow me."

She nodded nervously and followed the man through the tall dark halls. Her earlier impression of the place being a castle was further confirmed as she took in the décor and overall feel of the massive home. There was nothing cozy or lived-in about Dominic's house. It felt more like a museum than a place to live. It was beautiful, but it had no heart.

They arrived at the veranda. "Ms. Clayborn, sir," the man presented.

"Gemma!" Dominic exclaimed, coming toward her. "You've arrived."

He took her hand in his, raised it to his mouth, and kissed it lightly. He held it near his face and locked his eyes on hers, a sly smile turning up the corners of his bowed mouth.

"You are so beautiful. You take my breath away," he whispered.

Gemma tugged on her hand, and he finally released

it. Forcing herself to smile, she replied, "Thank you, Dominic. You're too kind. Really."

"Dinner is served, sir," the man in the tuxedo said.

"Thank you, Geoffrey," Dominic said with a wave of his hand. "Shall we?"

He offered his arm, and Gemma took it reluctantly. She reminded herself to breathe, forced her racing heartbeat to slow, and commanded the butterflies in her stomach to cease and desist. She knew what she planned to do was dangerous, but she also knew she had no choice but to see it through. There was no backing down.

Trying to make conversation, she asked, "How long ago was this house built? It's beautiful."

"This place has been in our family forever," he answered. "It was built not too long after your home, as a matter of fact."

"Really? That's fascinating," she replied.

"It was built by my great-great-grandfather. He was the mayor of Beacon Shores, you know," Dominic bragged.

"No, I didn't know. How lovely." She smiled, feigning ignorance.

"His name was Dogan. An extraordinary man, actually," he continued.

Gemma nodded, half listening but mostly reveling

in the fact that Dogan was the one who had built the house. It made her feel like she was on the right path, like she had a better chance of finding the spell book in the home built by Dogan himself.

They arrived at the grand dining room, and Dominic pulled out Gemma's chair, waited for her to sit, and then took the seat next to her, at the head of the immense table. Maids and butlers served the meal on silver trays with a flourish and a dash of flair. She had no doubt that he enjoyed displaying his wealth and power, and she decided to play into it, letting him believe she was as impressed as he wanted her to be.

After they had eaten their six-course meal, Gemma politely placed her cloth napkin on the fine bone china plate. "Dominic, that was delicious. Really. I can't remember the last time I dined like this."

"I'm so happy I could share it with you. You're a remarkable woman, after all. I consider myself a lucky man to be able to have a meal with you," he flattered. "And to talk with you about my desire to purchase Moonstone House, of course."

"Well, I would love to talk about your offer, but I need to find the little girls' room first." She smiled sweetly.

"Of course. It's just down the hall, the seventh door on the right," he replied.

"Second door?"

"No, seventh." He chuckled.

"Seventh. Right." She pushed her chair away from the table and stood. "I'll return shortly, and we can have our little chat."

"Wonderful. It's a lovely evening. How about I have the staff serve our after-dinner drinks on the veranda? We can talk there."

"Perfect. I'll join you after I powder my nose." She gave him a little wave and headed out of the dining room.

Her heels clicked on the stone floor as she quickly made her way down the long hallway. Glancing in each room as she passed, she tried to figure out where she should look. There was a coatroom, a solarium, and a sitting room. Finally, she came to one that looked like a study. The room was mostly dark, but there was a small desk lamp that had been left on.

"Bingo!" she whispered.

Glancing behind her to make sure no one was watching, Gemma quickly ducked into the room. Moving as fast as she could, she looked around the space. It appeared to be an office, and she was willing to bet money that it was Dominic's. If the spell book was going to be anywhere, she had a feeling it was in that room. Rowan said Dominic would keep it close to him. Dominic was a businessman, so his office seemed the obvious choice.

Gemma ran her fingers across the vast array of old books lining the shelf behind the desk. Nothing looked like a spell book, not that she really knew what one looked like. Turning around, she began to rifle through the desk, making sure she returned everything exactly the way she'd found it. She quickly pulled open each drawer, shuffled through the contents, and came up empty. Crouching down, she opened the bottom drawer of the desk. There it was! Her breath caught when she saw it.

The book was very old. It was bound in leather, and the front cover had the letters DB embossed on it. The thing looked like it might disintegrate at the slightest touch. She carefully opened the cover and skimmed a couple pages. It was written in a language that she'd come to recognize as German, thanks to the book she'd found. However, the latter pages were written in English.

"This has to be it," she murmured.

Sliding the book inside her handbag, she closed the desk drawer and quickly slipped out of the room. Pushing down her nervousness, she continued down the hall until she found the bathroom. She went inside, flipped on the light, and locked the door behind her.

Collapsing against the wall, she closed her eyes and took a few breaths until her heart stopped racing.

"I did it! I have Dogan Becker's spell book!" she whispered.

Knowing she'd been gone far too long, she made a show of flushing the toilet and washing her hands. Composing herself, she opened the bathroom door, screaming when she saw Dominic standing there, leaning against the wall.

"Did I scare you, Gemma?" he asked, his voice several degrees chillier than earlier.

"No... er, yes. I mean, I guess I didn't expect you to be standing outside the bathroom when I opened the door." She attempted a laugh.

Dominic looked at her carefully, a strange glint in his eyes. "You've been gone a very long time. I thought I should come and check on you."

"Oh, yeah, I'm sorry. I, uh... I'm not feeling so well." She put her hand on her stomach to underscore her point.

"I see." He continued to stare at her, his cold eyes making her skin crawl.

"So, uh, anyway, I'm really sorry, Dominic, but I think I need to go."

She took a step forward, but he didn't move, effectively blocking her path.

"So soon? We haven't even had a chance to have our chat."

"I know, and I'm terribly sorry. I have a, uh, a sensitive stomach. It's really embarrassing, but sometimes rich food just doesn't agree with me. I think I need to get home right away."

He stared at her for several more seconds, and Gemma held her breath.

"I'm sorry to hear that, Gemma. I was so looking forward to our conversation." He took her by the elbow and led her down the hallway.

"I know. Me too. Can we reschedule?"

"Of course, of course. As soon as you feel better."

They reached the end of the hall and stood in the entryway beside the massive front door.

"I'm sure I'll be doing much better by tomorrow. It never lasts long," she answered.

"Well, we'll be in touch, then," he said as he opened the door for her. "Would you like my driver to take you home since you're not feeling well? It's no problem at all."

"Oh no, that won't be necessary. I'm not that far away. I'll be home soon, and I can just crawl into bed and sleep this off." She plastered a congenial smile on her face.

"If you're sure."

"I'm sure. Thank you for dinner, Dominic. It was delicious, really. And we'll reschedule for another time, yes?"

"You can count on it, Gemma. I'll be seeing you soon."

On shaking legs, she walked down the front steps, opened the car door, and slid inside. Giving Dominic one final wave, she pulled out of the driveway and headed toward home.

"You have no idea who you're messing with, Dominic Becker," she said aloud, steel in her voice. "You, sir, have met your match."

Thirty-Three

Gemma pulled into her driveway, locked her car, and went inside the house. She hated coming home in the dark, so she'd left several lights on before she'd gone to Dominic's. Closing the front door behind her, she locked it up tightly, just as she'd promised Eric she would. She checked the other doors and windows downstairs for good measure, and after deciding everything was secure, she headed upstairs.

Dropping her handbag onto the bed, she reached inside and took out the spell book. It felt icy cold to the touch, which, strangely, she hadn't noticed earlier. The book was so cold, in fact, that if she hadn't known better, she'd have thought it had been stored in the freezer.

"So weird," she muttered.

Gemma placed the book on the bed and headed into the bathroom to shower. She stood under the hot water, shivering. She turned up the heat a bit more until the entire bathroom was filled with steam. Still, she couldn't seem to get warm, so she turned off the water and grabbed a towel. Trembling, she quickly dried off and put on flannel pajamas and thick wool socks, but she still couldn't seem to raise her body temperature.

Gemma jumped in her bed, slipped under the down comforter, and pulled it up to her chin, but still no luck. She was chilled to the bone. She saw the spell book lying there, and curiosity got the best of her. Sitting up, she grabbed the book and forced herself to ignore the shivering. The old book was freezing; it was like holding a chunk of ice in her hands. Her whole body felt numb.

Bending her stiff fingers, Gemma tried to flip through the pages, but the book didn't seem to want to open. She finally managed to turn to a page, but when she looked at it, she saw it was written in German. She did her best to open it toward the back cover, hoping to read some of the pages written in English, but it wouldn't budge.

"What good is this thing going to do me if I can't

even read it?" she said through her chattering teeth. "And why am I so cold?"

All at once, the room began to spin, and flashes of images played like a movie reel in her mind. The images were blurry and almost too fast to decipher, but she managed to catch a glimpse of the same woman she'd dreamed about in the barn, the one she'd learned was Pearl. Gemma saw her being dragged from the front porch of Moonstone House. She saw blips of a rope being tied and quick flashes of the redbud tree, its bright flowers falling from the branches like snow.

She heard a scream and realized it was her own.

Gemma covered her nose as a putrid, decaying smell emanated from the spell book. She dropped it quickly as it burned her hands. The cover felt like it was on fire. The smell of smoke filled the room, mixing with the overwhelming scent of death. Coughing, she covered her face with the down comforter. She gagged as the smell wafted through the air.

All at once, she heard the girl's haunting voice singing the strange song. Panic set in as Gemma broke out in a cold sweat. Pushing down nausea, fumbling for her phone, she tried to dial Eric's number, but the screen flashed the words "No Service."

Gemma heard the crunch of gravel, and a glint of headlights flashed through the window from the driveway below. Relieved that Eric was home, she sprang from the bed and ran downstairs as quickly as her trembling body would carry her. Sprinting through the kitchen, she twisted the doorknob, wanting nothing more than to throw herself into his arms and beg him to tell her she was going to be okay.

Tears ran down her cheeks as she flung open the front door. "I'm so glad you're—"

But it wasn't Eric. Instead, Dominic Becker stood before her with a look on his face that was so cold and evil it caused her knees to buckle.

A woman's voice screamed in her ear, "Run!"

Gemma tried to force her legs to move, but they seemed to be buried in concrete.

"I believe you have something that belongs to me," Dominic said icily.

Gemma's legs finally remembered how to move, and she took one step backward, attempting to run, but it was too late. Dominic reached out and grabbed her by the shoulders. She tried to fight back, but he was far too strong. He wrapped both of his large hands around her delicate neck and squeezed.

The room grew dark.

Thirty-Four

Eric turned up the radio and hummed along while Don Henley and the Eagles sang "Desperado." He'd made the trip to Deep River, and the windowpanes were safely tucked inside the back of the truck. The trip had taken a bit longer than he'd hoped, but he was making good time. He was less than half an hour away from Beacon Shores.

He chuckled to himself when he thought about how much he'd missed Gemma. He'd only been away from her for a few hours, but to him, it felt like years. He was so hooked on that woman it wasn't even funny.

"You're pathetic, man," he said aloud.

He'd called her earlier, before he'd left Deep River, but she hadn't answered. He imagined she'd been busy writing, and he hoped it was coming along well. Eric knew how much writing that book meant to her. He had faith in her. He knew she could do anything.

He turned up the song a bit louder, but suddenly, there was nothing but static on the radio. A squealing sound blared in the cab of the truck, and he turned the knob quickly, killing the volume. All at once, the hairs on his arms began to prickle, and a tingle shot down his spine. He knew what that meant.

Turning his head slightly, he saw Emerald sitting in the passenger seat, a look of fear and worry on her wrinkled face.

"Drive faster," she commanded.

"What's wrong? Is Gemma okay?" he barked, pushing down on the gas pedal.

"She needs you. Now, Eric. You must get there faster."

"What's happening?" he pleaded, his heart racing.

"Our girl needs you. Get to her. Now!"

Eric jammed the gas pedal to the floor, and the truck raced down the dark country road toward Moonstone House.

Thirty-Five

Opal groaned and rolled over in bed. She covered her head with the pillow and tried to drown out the voice that was trying to wake her.

"Get up," the voice said. "Opal!"

Pulling the pillow off her head, she sat up. Moonlight filtered in through the curtains of the Davises' spare bedroom. She glanced around the room, confused. Someone had been talking to her, telling her to wake up. Whoever it was had even called her by name.

Slipping out of bed, she crept to the door and opened it. Glancing down the hallway, she saw no one. It was very late at night, and everyone was asleep, so who had been talking to her?

Going back inside the room, she stopped. There it was again.

"Opal!"

Creeping to the closet, she opened the door. Of course, it was empty. She walked over to the window, pushed the curtains aside, and looked out. Standing on the sidewalk was the girl from the woods, Ruby. Confused, Opal stared at her. Ruby waved her arms around, motioning for Opal to come outside.

She threw on a hoodie with her pajama bottoms, slid her feet into her Doc Martens, and quietly slipped through the hall, down the stairs, and out the front door.

"What are you doing here?" Opal asked.

"I came for you," Ruby replied.

"How did you know I was here? I don't understand." She shook her head in confusion.

"That doesn't matter. You have to come with me now," the girl demanded.

"I barely know you. Why do you think I would come with you?" Opal retorted.

"You're going to have to trust me."

"Give me one good reason." Opal put her hands on her hips and stared the girl down.

"Because your mother needs you. She's in danger. Now stop asking questions and follow me."

Opal's heart leaped into her throat, and she nodded in understanding. Something about the urgency in Ruby's voice convinced Opal she was telling the truth, even though it made no logical sense. Ruby took off running, and Opal followed, right on her heels.

As they ran, Ruby repeated a prayer over and over again until Opal knew the words by heart. "Lord Jesus, thy wounds so red will guard me against death. Amen."

Opal ran until her lungs felt like they were on fire. A million questions swam in her brain, and she didn't have a single answer to any of them. One thing she knew for certain—Ruby, whoever she was, was not a normal girl.

Thirty-Six

Gemma's eyes flew open, and she gasped for breath, feeling as if her lungs would never be full again. She tried to sit up, but she couldn't. Working to move her arms, she quickly figured out that they, along with her legs, were bound tightly. She wriggled her body, trying to break free, but the effort was in vain. The ropes burned against her flesh as she tried to free herself. It was no use. She couldn't move.

Forcing herself to lie still, she looked around, desperate to get her bearings. She was lying on the ground, staring up at the redbud tree. The red flowers swayed in the wind, and she could have sworn that they were whispering, "Don't be afraid."

Gemma heard a sound and noticed Dominic

standing next to the tree, muttering under his breath. In his hands was a thick, long rope. Her blood turned to ice in her veins when she realized what he was doing —tying the rope into a noose.

"It didn't have to come to this," he said to her. "If you had just done what I told you to do, none of this would have happened."

The look on his face was one of insanity and rage. He was clearly a man on a mission, and while she believed he was past the point of reason, she knew she had to try.

"Dominic, please. I'm sorry. I can be really stubborn, you know. I'll listen to you now. I'll do anything you want me to do. Just untie me," she pleaded.

"It's too late for that."

"No, it isn't too late. It can't be too late. Please, Dominic," she begged.

"I have to put an end to this. I have to," he mumbled, continuing to tie the knot in the rope.

"Please," she cried. "Let me go."

"You must hang!" he screamed, his face contorting with rage. "Hang like the witch you are! Like the witches all the women in your family have always been!"

"But you're wrong," she sobbed. "We're not witches, and deep down, you know that."

"Hang the witch! Hang the witch! Hang the witch!" he chanted over and over again, oblivious to her pleas.

Gemma struggled with the ropes again, her skin burning as it rubbed against the rough twine. Dominic wasn't going to listen to her, and she was running out of time and options. She closed her eyes and tried to focus, tried to come up with a plan. Nothing came.

Sobbing quietly, Gemma pictured Opal's face. How had it come to this? She couldn't leave her daughter. She just couldn't. Opal had no family other than Gemma. She thought of her mother, Topaz. They hadn't always seen eye to eye, but she had loved her fiercely. Then she pictured Grandma Emerald. She imagined her kind face.

Suddenly, Gemma saw a line of women standing side by side, shoulder to shoulder. The line started with Topaz and ended with the woman she'd come to know as Pearl. They were the women of her family line —the Jewels.

Pearl stepped out of the line and walked over to Gemma. Dropping to her knees, Pearl wiped the tears from Gemma's face. "Don't be afraid. We're here with you. All of us."

"But I'm going to die," Gemma cried. "I'm not ready to die."

Quietly Pearl began to speak. "Cross of Christ and Crown of Christ and Jesus Christ; red blood, be to me at all times and all hours good. God the Father is before me. God the Son is at my side. God the Holy Ghost is behind me. Who now is stronger than these three persons may come to seize me?"

Pearl paused and then spoke again, louder. "Cross of Christ and Crown of Christ and Jesus Christ; red blood, be to me at all times and all hours good. God the Father is before me. God the Son is at my side. God the Holy Ghost is behind me. Who now is stronger than these three persons may come to seize me?"

Soon, all the women in the line spoke the words with Pearl over and over again. All at once, a sense of peace washed over Gemma. It was a feeling of tranquility that she couldn't explain. She closed her eyes and ignored the fact that she was tied up and that Dominic was preparing a noose for her hanging. Nothing mattered except the sweet words the women kept repeating.

Thirty-Seven

Eric raced toward Moonstone House, pushing his truck far past the limit of safety. He didn't care. Nothing mattered except getting to Gemma. A deep, primal fear seeped into his gut. It was bad. He could feel it. The culmination of hundreds of years' worth of pain and suffering had reached the boiling point. It would be finished soon, one way or another.

"Faster, Eric. She needs you," Emerald whispered, tears streaming down her cheeks.

"Tell me she's going to be okay. After all of this, all we've done, she has to be, right?" he asked, his voice cracking with emotion.

"Good always wins in the end, Eric. But it often

comes at a price. And things seldom end the way we want them to," Emerald said cryptically.

Eric begged his truck to go faster. He was only a mile away from Moonstone House, but he might as well have been on the other side of the world. He felt Gemma slipping away from him every second, and there was nothing he could do about it.

Thirty-Eight

Ruby ran as fast as a deer, and Opal did her best to keep up.

"Lord Jesus, thy wounds so red will guard me against death. Amen," Ruby continued to pray.

They kept running until they reached the woods next to Moonstone House. Ruby stopped quickly to catch her breath. Opal did the same, panting and sucking in air.

Turning to Opal, Ruby said, "We need to cut through the woods. We'll get there faster that way."

Opal shook her head slowly from side to side. She hadn't been in the woods since the day she'd been almost attacked by the group of guys from school. She had been too afraid to go back. She hated herself for it, but it was the truth.

"I don't think I can," Opal squeaked.

"Yes you can. Your mother needs you," Ruby insisted.

"But—"

"Opal, you have nothing to fear in those woods as long as you're with me. Now let's go!" Ruby commanded as she sprinted into the dark forest, leaving Opal little choice but to follow.

Nodding quickly in agreement, Opal took off after her.

Thirty-Nine

"It's time," Dominic commanded.

He reached down and grabbed Gemma's small body, hoisting her to her feet. She wobbled, partially from dizziness but also because her hands and feet were tied. She had no way to balance herself.

"Get up there." Dominic motioned toward a stool he'd placed beneath the lowest branch of the redbud tree.

Gemma gave no response. She didn't move, didn't speak, and didn't comply.

Groaning with anger and frustration, Dominic picked her up as if she weighed no more than a feather and placed her feet on the stool, forcing her to stand. He climbed the ladder that he'd placed next to the stool and attached the rope to the lowest branch, securing it tightly. He then draped the end of the rope around Gemma's neck, tightening the knot behind her ear.

She didn't cry, and she didn't beg for her life. She refused to give Dominic Becker the satisfaction of her tears.

Dominic placed his face directly in front of Gemma's, and she stared him down. She could see the anger bubbling behind his eyes. He wanted her to be afraid. He wanted her to beg him to spare her life. He couldn't stand the fact that she wouldn't.

Roughly, he put his hand behind her head and shoved her face toward his. His cold lips pressed hard against hers, and she forced herself to push down the bile that rose in her stomach. He kissed her angrily, running his hands greedily up and down her body. She stood perfectly still, not reacting.

Unsatisfied, he pulled himself away from her and yanked a white cloth over her head, covering her face.

"It's a shame I have to do this to you. Really, it is," he spat.

With her head covered, Gemma had no idea what was happening. Fear finally overtook her, and her body began to tremble uncontrollably. She bit back sobs, knowing her very life was about to slip away from her.

All Dominic had to do was move the stool from beneath her feet and she was gone.

Pearl's voice began whispering in her ear once again. "Cross of Christ and Crown of Christ and Jesus Christ; red blood, be to me at all times and all hours good. God the Father is before me. God the Son is at my side. God the Holy Ghost is behind me. Who now is stronger than these three persons may come to seize me?"

Soon, Gemma raised her voice and joined in, speaking the words loudly. Her fear was gone.

Dominic stood below her, chanting, "Thou shalt not suffer a witch to live," over and over again like a mantra.

Gemma ignored him, speaking the words Pearl kept whispering in her ear, forcing her voice to be louder than Dominic's.

Finally, Dominic stopped speaking. Gemma followed suit. Taking a deep breath, she decided she would try to reason with him one more time.

"Dominic, please listen to me. I'm not a witch. You know very well that I'm not."

"Silence, witch!" he screamed, kicking the stool.

It wobbled slightly, and Gemma felt the rope tighten around her neck. Pushing down the fear, she tried again. "I understand why you're doing this. I know this isn't what you want. I know all about the witchcraft curse that Dogan passed down to your family. This curse isn't your fault."

Dominic laughed loudly, a wild, crazy sound that chilled Gemma to the bone. "Curse? You know nothing! This isn't a curse. What Dogan passed down was a gift! Do you have any idea how powerful I am? And I'll be even more powerful as soon as I rid this town of the blight of your family once and for all!"

"Dominic, you don't want to do this," she said again.

"If Pearl had listened when Dogan told her to go away, none of this would have happened. She knew the rules. Brauchers don't share territories. There's only room for one of us here, Gemma, and it isn't you."

Forty

Gemma gasped as the sound of gravel crunching beneath tires echoed in the night. She heard a car door slam and the pounding sound of running footsteps.

Dominic cursed under his breath. He reached up and wrapped his hands around her leg, tightening them like a vise. Gemma's breath came in rapid spurts. She knew all he had to do was move the stool and she would die.

"Let her go, Dominic," Eric screamed. "This is over."

"It's not over, you fool," Dominic screeched. "It's just beginning!"

Gemma tried to make her body still as a statue. She understood that the less she moved, the less she struggled against him, the more likely it was that she could stay alive. Over and over she repeated the words that Pearl kept whispering in her ear.

"Don't come any closer, Eric, or she's dead," Dominic yelled, wiggling the stool beneath Gemma's feet for effect.

"Eric, please, listen to him. I don't want to die," Gemma sobbed.

"I mean what I'm saying, Eric. The witch dies tonight!" Dominic taunted.

Suddenly a strange voice shouted in the distance. Everyone grew silent, and the voice gained in volume and intensity.

"Lord Jesus, thy wounds so red will guard me against death. Lord Jesus, thy wounds so red will guard me against death. Lord Jesus, thy wounds so red will guard me against death."

The voice grew louder as the speaker came closer.

"Mom," Opal screamed.

Her daughter's voice caused Gemma's heart to seize.

"Opal, do not come any closer. You need to leave. Now!" she yelled.

"I'm not leaving you," Opal shrieked.

"Leave!" Dominic bellowed. "If you come any

closer, I'll kill her now. And you're next! I'm done messing around."

Gemma couldn't see what was happening, but she heard the sound of footsteps coming closer. Dominic's grip on her leg tightened.

"I know who you are," said the stranger's voice. "You're the coward descendant of the man who killed my mother."

Gemma gasped as understanding dawned. Although she didn't know how it was possible, she knew the person talking had to be one of Pearl's daughters.

"You're nothing but a child." Dominic laughed derisively. "Your power is no match for mine."

"Perhaps," the girl replied. "I may not be powerful enough on my own, but the three of us together, well, you're no match for us."

Dominic gasped and loosened his hold on Gemma's leg.

"I believe you know my mother, Pearl, and my sister, Amethyst," the girl said forcefully. "We have come to finish this."

Forty-One

Gemma's heart pounded, her body rigid and on high alert. Although she couldn't see what was happening, she felt waves of fear coming off Dominic's body.

"Lord Jesus, thy wounds so red will guard me against death," the group of women repeated in unison.

Three loud cracks of thunder ripped through the sky, and Gemma jumped. Still, the women repeated the words. Gemma heard Dominic swear as he released his grip on her. Suddenly, the cover was lifted off her head, and she saw Eric's tear-streaked face next to hers.

Sobbing, Opal ran to them, and together, Eric and Opal untied Gemma's hands and feet. When she was free, Eric lifted her off the stool and cradled her to his chest. Opal wrapped her arms around both of them, and the three clung to one another like drowning people to a life raft.

Eric gently set Gemma on her feet, and she turned her head toward the commotion across the yard. Shocked, she saw Dominic on his knees, surrounded by three women—Pearl and both of her daughters.

"Please, please spare my life," Dominic begged them. "Mercy. Please."

Pearl raised her voice and spoke with authority. "Revelation 20 verses 1 and 2 say, 'And I saw an angel come down from heaven, having the key of the bottomless pit and a great chain in his hand. And he laid hold of the dragon, that old serpent, which is the Devil, and Satan, and bound him a thousand years.'"

Dominic trembled, cowering beneath Pearl's stern gaze.

"Gemma," Pearl called to her. "Please go into the house and get the scissors."

Confused, Gemma complied. She ran into the kitchen, fumbled through the drawers, and grabbed the kitchen shears. Running back outside, she offered them to Pearl.

"This is for you to do, Gemma," Pearl said with a smile. "Cut a lock of his hair."

With trembling hands, Gemma grabbed a chunk

of Dominic's hair and chopped it off. She wrapped it in her fist and awaited further instruction.

"Go inside and get the spell book," Pearl told her.

Gemma forced her trembling legs to run up the stairs, grab the book, and return to Pearl.

"Now place the lock of his hair inside the spell book," Pearl said.

Gemma flipped the book open and placed Dominic's black hair inside. Slamming it shut, she looked at Pearl.

"Eric, go get the shovel," Pearl said next.

Nodding quickly, Eric ran to the barn and returned in a flash, shovel in hand.

"Amethyst, show him the spot," Pearl said to the oldest of her daughters.

Amethyst walked to the redbud tree and pointed at the ground. "Here. Dig here," she instructed.

Forty-Two

Eric jammed the shovel into the dirt and began digging, upending pile after pile of earth. He dug down deep, stopping only when the shovel hit something hard. Crouching to his knees, he reached into the ground and pulled out a large wooden box.

"Set it aside for now," Pearl commanded.

Eric nodded and placed the box on the ground next to the redbud tree.

"Gemma, put the spell book with the lock of hair into the hole," Amethyst said to her.

Gemma kneeled to the ground and did as she was told. After placing the book into the hole, she stood to her feet.

Pearl and the younger daughter walked over to where they were gathered.

"Now, cover it with dirt, six feet underground," Pearl said.

Eric grabbed the shovel and filled in the hole, then patted the earth until it was flat.

Dominic, who was still crouched on the ground, began to whimper.

Pearl's voice, filled with intensity and authority, spoke into the stillness of the night. "Two wicked eyes have overshadowed me, but three other eyes are overshadowing me too, one of God the Father, another of God the Son, and the third of God the Holy Spirit. They watch my blood and flesh, my marrow and bone. I am protected in the name of God."

Dominic began to screech, his voice shrill. He curled into a ball and screamed, "No! Leave me alone!"

Pearl spoke the words again, this time joined by her daughters. When they had finished, Pearl commanded, "You must leave now. You no longer hold any power here."

They began to speak. "In God's name I call upon three angels: the first to protect me, the other to destroy all weapons against me, the third to keep my soul."

When he heard the words, Dominic jumped to his

feet and ran like a streak of lightning. He jumped into his car, started the ignition, and screeched out of the driveway, gravel spitting beneath the quickly rotating tires.

Gemma, watching him go and realizing it was over, collapsed on the ground and sobbed.

Forty-Three

Gemma sat on the ground crying for what seemed like an eternity, Opal curled beside her, her head resting on her mother's lap.

"I was so scared when I saw you there like that, Mom," Opal said, her voice shaking with emotion. "I don't know what I would do if I lost you."

"You're not going to. I promise," Gemma said softly, stroking Opal's hair gently.

"You've done it, Gemma. Just as we always knew you would," Pearl said with a smile, helping both Opal and Gemma to their feet.

"You... you're...," Opal stammered, looking at Ruby.

"I'm Ruby, Pearl's youngest daughter," the girl explained. "I've been watching over you."

"But I don't understand," Opal replied. "If you're Pearl's daughter, how are you here? You'd be, like, a hundred years old."

"Yes," Gemma chimed in. "None of this makes any sense."

"I'll explain," Pearl began. "The winter after the town epidemic, the people of Beacon Shores decided I was the cause of all their problems. They stopped buying my tinctures, my wares, and stopped coming to me as a healer."

"They cut us off," Amethyst added.

"We were shunned," Ruby stated.

"I was so angry. I was afraid for my daughters. I didn't know how we would survive, cut off from the town like that. So, when the mayor's wife told me we were no longer welcome in town, I did a terrible thing —I cursed the town. I told them they would pay for our mistreatment. When the fire came and the town burned, naturally they believed it was my doing." Pearl shrugged.

"Was it?" Gemma asked.

"Of course not," Pearl said sadly. "But the damage was already done. Dogan Becker led that mob to Moonstone House. They were in a frenzy, screaming, 'Hang the witch.' They wouldn't listen to reason.

They dragged me from my house and hanged me, right there in the redbud tree."

"Just like Dominic tried to do to me." Gemma shivered.

"Yes. I told the town that because of the wrong they had done to me, Beacon Shores would burn again." Pearl shook her head sadly. "If only I had known the harm those words would do."

"That was the most terrible night of our lives," Amethyst said. "Or so I believed at the time."

"What could be worse than that?" Opal asked.

"I was only eighteen years old when Mama died, and Ruby was just nine. We were afraid, but we learned pretty quickly how to make the best of our situation. We were orphans. Ruby became my responsibility. We learned to fend for ourselves. The next year, I got married. My husband was a kind man who was more than happy to help me take care of Ruby," Amethyst recalled. "I also had a child by that time, a little girl named Crystal."

"So everything turned out all right, then," Opal said.

"Not exactly," Ruby replied, a look of sadness covering her face.

"Six years passed, and we thought everything was fine. Then, one terrible night, Beacon Shores burned again. Dogan never let the town forget my mother's words, so naturally, they blamed Pearl's daughters for the fire," Amethyst mused. "Once again, Dogan led an angry mob to Moonstone House."

"No," Opal breathed.

"I'm afraid so. My husband and I hid Crystal in the jelly closet while we stayed and attempted to reason with them. Ruby was fast and comfortable in the woods, so I told her to run there," Amethyst answered, tears falling from her eyes. "Looking back, I should have kept her hidden with my daughter."

"I ran as fast as I could, but there were too many of them. Fortunately, I led them away from the house, so my sister and niece were safe," Ruby said quietly. "They caught up to me on the bridge in the woods."

"The bridge where I met you?" Opal asked, her forehead wrinkling with confusion.

"Yes." Ruby nodded. "The men attacked me. They killed me that night and threw my body into the creek. I was just fifteen years old."

"And that's—" Opal began.

"That's why I'm still here," Ruby finished. "I've been stuck, with no way to get closure. Until now."

Forty-Four

Everything was silent. No one breathed a word, each one trying to digest the pieces of the story the women told.

Finally, Opal spoke. "What about the box? What's inside?"

"You'll find out when Gemma opens it," Pearl answered with a smile.

Gemma walked over to the box and inspected it closely. Crouching down, she ran her fingers over the lid. "How am I supposed to open it? Where's the key?"

"You already have the key," Ruby revealed with a grin.

Something about her voice sparked a memory inside Gemma's mind. "It's you. The song. It's you."

Smiling, Ruby opened her mouth and began to

sing, the sound causing the hairs on Gemma's arms to stand on end.

"Listen close and you'll find me,
Buried 'neath the Remembering Tree.
Tucked inside and nestled deep,
Buried 'neath the Remembering Tree.
Hearts of hatred, hearts of greed
Seek the treasure buried deep.
Only she who holds the key
Will unearth the secrets of the Remembering Tree."

When Ruby finished the song, Gemma took off running. She tore through the kitchen, ran up the stairs, threw open the dresser drawer, and grabbed the skeleton key. Sprinting down the stairs, she went back outside. Dropping to her knees, she placed the key into the rusty lock. It clicked.

Gemma lifted the lid, and it creaked open. She gasped when she saw what was inside. It was piled high, packed full of the largest gems and jewels she had ever seen.

"How... what... are these... are they real?" she squeaked.

"They are definitely real." Pearl laughed.

"But this box must be worth a fortune! And it was

buried in the ground?" Gemma questioned. "How long has it been there?"

"It's been there for many years, my dear," Pearl said, patting Gemma's arm. "It was given to me by one of the great loves of my life."

"Sterling?" Gemma asked.

"Yes. Sterling Eric Johnson," she said with a grin.

"My great-great-grandfather," Eric added.

"So you've known all along?" Gemma asked, the pieces coming together.

Eric nodded and winked at her.

"Sterling and I loved each other very much, but because of what he was and what I was, we knew our time together would be short-lived. But his love for me was so great that he found a way to keep our connection. His descendants have been watching over mine, protecting them, for over a hundred years," Pearl explained.

Eric reached out and took Gemma's hands in his. Squeezing them tightly, he looked into her eyes. She found herself swimming in the blue of them, just as she had the first time she'd seen him. She'd known in that moment that they were somehow connected, partnered, joined together across time, defying all logic.

"When I told you I had been waiting for you for a

hundred years, I meant it." He smiled. "I love you, Gemma. Across lifetimes, I've always loved you."

"And I love you," she replied with tears in her eyes.

"So, what happens now? What about all these jewels?" Opal asked, gesturing toward the box.

"They're your mother's. She can do with them what she wishes." Pearl shrugged. "They were given to me to take care of my family, and that's what they'll do."

Pearl, Ruby, and Amethyst joined hands. Gemma and Opal also joined hands and faced them.

"You saved my life, you know," Gemma said to them.

"No, my dear. You saved your own. Your bravery and refusal to give up are what saved you. You broke the curse. You're the one who saved us all," Pearl answered.

Pearl and her daughters began to grow fuzzy, fading in and out of focus. Gemma wasn't sure what was happening, but she wasn't ready to let them go.

"Pearl, don't go. Come back," Gemma said, her head spinning.

The women's forms became hazy, and Gemma's eyes worked hard to focus. The women were blinking in and out like static on a television station with a bad signal. The roar of the ocean in her ears was deafening. The women were disappearing.

Spinning around in circles, Gemma looked for them, but they were gone. Everyone was gone.

Had they ever been there at all? Were they real? Was any of this real?

Squeezing her pounding head between her palms, Gemma screamed as the ground came up to meet her.

Forty-Five

"Mom, Mom, wake up. Please." Opal's voice echoed somewhere in the distance.

"Gemma," came another voice, a man's. "Gemma, open your eyes. You're all right."

Gemma blinked a few times, glancing around as her daughter's face swam into her line of vision. She moved her hands, feeling prickling blades of grass beneath her palms.

"Wh-what happened? Why am I on the ground?" she stammered, sitting up slowly.

"You passed out," the man said, reaching out to pull her to her feet. "How are you feeling?"

"I'm okay. Did I really pass out?" She shook her head, trying to remember what had happened.

"You did, Mom," Opal answered, worry echoing in her voice.

"I don't remember anything at all. I shook your hand, and then everything just got all fuzzy," she replied, confused.

"You probably need to eat something. Your blood sugar might be low," Opal offered, sounding much wiser than her years. "Plus, we've been driving all day."

"Are you sure you're okay?" the man inquired, compassion and worry washing over his handsome face.

"Yeah, I think I am. I feel just fine now."

"You were out for a couple minutes. I was starting to worry that I might need to call someone," the man said.

"I know you, don't I? At least I think I do. You're the contractor, right?" Gemma looked at the kind man closely, trying to remember what he'd said his name was.

"I am." He smiled.

"Eric Johnson," she stated, as the memory resurfaced. "That's what you told me your name was right before I passed out."

"Guilty as charged." He chuckled.

"Well, Eric Johnson, that was quite an introduction. I mean, do women always fall at your feet?" Gemma smiled, trying for a joke in order to lighten the moment.

"Not quite like that," he answered with a hearty laugh.

Gemma cleared her throat. "Well, like I started to say, I'm Gemma." She nodded toward her daughter. "And this is Opal, my daughter."

"Nice to meet you both." Eric grinned. "Welcome to Moonstone House. I've been waiting for you."

Gemma looked across the yard at Moonstone House. It seemed crazy, but she could swear she heard a sigh of relief, as if the house itself had been holding its breath, waiting for her return. She blinked twice, certain her eyes were playing tricks on her. She saw a shimmering image of a strange yet familiar woman sitting in her grandmother's rocking chair, flanked by a young woman on one side and a teenage girl on the other.

"We're always with you," they said together.

The strangest sense of déjà vu came over Gemma, almost as if it had all happened before, somewhere once upon a dream.

Finally, she settled her gaze on the beautiful redbud tree in the front yard. It was in full bloom, the lush red flowers swaying in the breeze. She listened closely, and as she did, the tree whispered to her.

"Welcome home," it said.

Looking for more unique suspenses from HR Mason? Check out **Nothing Hidden Ever Stays.**

Acknowledgments

I would first like to thank my publisher, Tangled Tree Publishing, for their amazing support. They never cease to amaze me at the way they listen to my wishes and preferences for my books. It's such a collaborative effort, and I am forever thankful for them. Next, I want to thank my amazing editor, Kristin. Her help and advice bring out the best in me and my work. I am also super thankful to Robert Phoenix, Braucher extraordinaire! His willingness to speak with me about the Braucheri traditions and customs made this book what it is. He is such a wealth of knowledge, and his desire to share that was so amazingly helpful. Finally, I want to thank my family and friends for always believing in me and supporting this crazy dream of mine. I couldn't do it without you.

About the Author

HR Mason is an Ohio girl transplanted into the Pacific Northwest. She is a people-watching introvert who can be found hiding out in the nearest corner. When not writing, she loves rainy days at the beach, old houses and antiques, researching family history, reading, and getting lost inside her own thoughts. She is a lover of caffeine and a hopeless romantic at heart. A multi-published author in the Romance genre, she moved into new writing territory in 2019 when she crossed genres. *Nothing Hidden Ever Stays*, her debut Gothic Suspense novel, became an Amazon bestseller. It was the winner of the American Fiction Award for Mystery/Suspense, as well as a Finalist in the Best Book Awards.

Join HR's reader group: www.facebook.com/groups/346156819065335/

twitter.com/heidireneemason

instagram.com/authorhrmason

bookbub.com/authors/hr-mason

About the Publisher

Tangled Tree Publishing loves all things tangled and aims to bring darker, twisted, and more mind-boggling books to its readers. Publishing adult and new adult fiction, TTPubs are all about diverse reads in mystery, suspense, thrillers, and crime.

For more details, head to WWW.TANGLEDTREEPUBLISHING.COM

facebook.com/tangledtreepublishing
twitter.com/ttpubs
instagram.com/hottreepublishing

THE REMEMBERING TREE

HR MASON

TANGLED TREE PUBLISHING